THE

NOVELIST

THE
NOVELIST

WILL OVERBY

OWENSBORO, KENTUCKY
2016

Copyright © 2016 William Overby

Cover Art:
Man: © Can Stock Photo Inc. / Sannie32
Tree: © Can Stock Photo Inc. / PinkBadger

ISBN-13: 978-1-945776-00-7
ISBN-10: 1-945776-00-5

I
Fireflies

THE APPEARANCE OF FIREFLIES during the first week of January should have been a hint to Lee Houston that his life was about to become strange. After all, the New Year had brought with it an intense cold, and the past three days had been below zero.

So when Corey came running through the den to the open French doors of Lee's study calling out, "Daddy! Come quick! Come look at all the fireflies!" Lee was sure his son was mistaken. That swamp gas from moldering logs was rising in the forested lot across the street, or – more likely – that the two redneck pre-teens from the next street over were creeping around in the woods with flashlights.

Lee slipped off his glasses and set them atop the manuscript he was reading. "It's not the right time of year for fireflies, buddy."

Corey turned his round eyes up to Lee. "Well, they're out there anyway."

Lee pulled Corey close and kissed him lightly on his downy blond hair. He smelled of Johnson's Baby Shampoo and Ivory soap, and the feet of his Pooh pajamas were stretched tight around his growing toes. "You've about outgrown these already."

Corey tugged at Lee's hand. "Come on, come see."

Lee blew out a breath and climbed out of his chair, arching his back as he followed Corey through the darkened house. God, his back hurt. How long had he been sitting there, anyway? And when did it get dark? "This better be good," he told Corey.

But Corey was already at the front door, holding it open to the blast of icy wind whipping through the foyer. He pointed outside. "See?"

Lee leaned against the doorframe, crossing his arms against the cold and squinting into the gloom. "I'll be damned."

There were hundreds of them, floating across the yard like illuminated snowflakes, flickering like candles, drifting through the bare limbs of the winter trees like fairies. He'd never seen anything like it. Weren't they supposed to go dormant or fly south for the winter or something? He stepped out onto the porch in his socks, barely aware of the icy concrete beneath his feet. This was crazy.

He looked down at Corey. "Go get your mom and sister. I think they're in the kitchen."

Corey took a last look at the fireflies and raced toward the back of the house, his steps pattering on the hardwood. He said something in that high excited voice of his, and soon Jessie and Lizbeth were following him down the hallway toward the front door.

"What's going on?" Jessie said, brushing a strand of dark hair from her eyes. "What's out there?"

"Fireflies," Lee said. He pointed out into the yard.

"Wow," Lizbeth said. She took hold of Jessie's arm and huddled against her from the cold.

Jessie put a hand on Lee's shoulder. He could feel the heat of her palm even through his sweater. "What do you make of that?" she said.

Lee shook his head. "Strangest thing I've ever seen."

"What do you think got them stirred up?"

"No idea."

They watched the spectacle in eerie silence for a few moments until the quiet was broken by a dog barking somewhere along the next block. Wood smoke had drifted along the street and now it pooled at the edge of the driveway, and the fireflies appeared as tiny lighthouses through a ghostly fog.

"It's so pretty," Corey said, waving his hand. "It's like Christmas."

Lizbeth snorted. "Christmas is over."

Lee thumped the back of Lizbeth's head with a knuckle. He knew they would bicker more as they got older, and he dreaded that. He hated to see them grow up, ached for them because they didn't know all the turmoil ahead of them. If he could only keep them like this, preserve them forever – Corey at seven and Lizbeth at twelve. But he pushed that from his mind. Time went fast enough without mourning what hadn't passed yet.

Macbeth, the gray cat, had slinked his way outside, and now he sat watching the spectacle as well, whiskers twitching and tail flicking. "What do you think, cat?"

Lee said.

"Can I go catch some?" Corey asked.

"You're already in your pajamas," Jessie said. "Besides, it's freezing out here. You'll catch your death."

Corey clasped his hands together and looked up at her. "Oh, please, Mom, please!"

"Come on, Jess," Lee said. "When are you ever going to see anything like this again?"

Jessie blew out a breath. "All right. I think I've got a jar in the pantry." She started back in the house. "But you kids at least put your boots and coats on."

In a few moments, Lee and Corey were stalking the fireflies through the darkened yard while Jessie and Lizbeth watched from the front steps. Lee held the empty Mason jar in one hand and the metal cap in the other, waiting to scoop up a bug and snap the lid on in one movement. He'd been pretty adept at catching fireflies when he was a kid, and he knew the way to get the best ones was to be slow and deliberate. No sudden movements – they didn't like that. He caught one – a big one – and squatted down so he and Corey could look at it. It crawled around inside the glass, blinking like a drunken neon sign.

"How do they turn on and off like that?" Corey asked, tapping at the jar.

Lee reached out and cupped another one in his palm, then gently snapped it into the jar. "They have a special chemical in their bodies that glows."

Corey watched the fireflies in the jar, his eyes round and shiny. "This is too cool. Winter fireflies."

"What the devil you got going on here, Houston?"

Lee looked up to see Ed Grant from down the street,

walking his little terrier and just barely illuminated by the street light. Ed, not a small man, looked like a bear in his heavy coat and wool hat. "Fireflies," Lee said. "Can you believe this?"

Ed shook his head and stared at the yard. "Where'd they come from?"

"Don't know," Lee said. "Corey happened to look outside and see 'em."

Ed grunted. "You must have something special in your yard. You still have that same lawn company come spray your grass every month?"

"Only in the summer." Lee looked at him. "Wait, are you saying these fireflies aren't anywhere else?"

"Nope. Me and Patches been up and down this whole block. Nowhere but here." He scratched his head underneath his cap and ran a finger across his bristly mustache. "Damnedest thing I've ever seen. Are they regular fireflies?"

Lee held up the jar for Ed to see. "They look normal to me. But there's something strange about them. I mean, it's ten degrees out here. Insects can't even function when it's this cold, can they?"

Ed shook his head. "Hell if I know. I barely passed Biology." He tilted his head toward the trees across the street. "Maybe something heated up part of the woods. A fire or something."

"I do smell smoke," Lee said, "but I figured it was somebody's woodstove. It's no stronger than usual."

Ed and Patches lumbered on down the street. "Got yourself a mystery there, Houston. Enjoy your lightnin' bugs." He and the dog slipped into the darkness and disappeared.

Lee looked back at Corey. "Let's go inside. I bet

dinner's almost ready and I can't feel my fingers."

*   *   *

After they had eaten and Cory was tucked into bed with the jar of fireflies on the nightstand beside him, Lee left Jessie and Lizbeth parked in front of the television in the den and returned to the solace of his study. The manuscript still lay as he had left it, dog-eared and scattered. He stared at it a moment, a knot forming in his stomach, then moved through the other door into the foyer and peered out the window. All the fireflies had gone now, leaving the front yard dark and empty. He switched off the porch lights and shuffled into the darkened living room. He needed a drink.

He pulled a bottle of bourbon from the liquor cabinet and glanced about the room. It was massive, really, with a yawning stone fireplace dominating one wall, flanked on either side by windows and French doors that led out to the back terrace. Jessie's baby grand piano sat in one corner, its lid closed to protect the delicate ivory keys. Two plush sofas and four chairs formed a conversation area in the center of the room, and on the wall opposite him the stereo shelf sat silent, his ample music collection hidden in the cabinets below. When they bought this house in the gated community of The Pines on the outskirts of the city, Lee and Jessie both fell in love with the size of this room, envisioning lavish parties where the food and drink overflowed to a bounty of guests, where Jessie would play cocktail music on the piano and Lee would tend the bar. But in the five years they had lived here there had only been two parties, both of them rather lackluster affairs, and Jessie hadn't touched the piano since it had been moved into the room.

The bar, however, was always in full operation. Jim Beam in hand, Lee headed down the dark hall to the kitchen. After rummaging through the cabinets, he filled a shaker a third full of orange juice, then added some ice and a healthy dose of bourbon. He shook it violently and poured it into a glass, then took a small sip and licked the foam from his upper lip. Perfect. Jessie hated this drink, which he called a "sunbeam," and she made the funniest faces when he drank one in front of her. "Way to ruin a good glass of orange juice," she always said.

He carried the drink back to the study and sat down at his desk, then opened up his internet browser. Fireflies in January? He Googled "winter fireflies" and followed links to several etymology sites. Certain species did in fact mate during the winter months, but nothing like the spectacle they had just witnessed on the front lawn. And never in the brutal cold like they were experiencing this year. It just didn't make sense. He started to close out of the browser but an entry farther down the page caught his eye.

Fireflies as a portent of death

He sipped his drink and clicked on the link.

Fireflies are sometimes seen as one of the portents of death, as described by the Dalai

Lama in his book, *Advice on Dying*. Many people believe the "fireflies" he describes are merely visual disturbances caused hypotension as a person's blood pressure drops just before death.

No. That couldn't be what they saw. These were real. They were in a jar upstairs in Corey's room. He shut down the computer and sat in the sudden silence. He'd deal with them more tomorrow. Right now he couldn't think. His mind was too befuddled.

He took a sip of his drink and eyed the yellowing sheets of paper spread out on the desk. He had pored over this same manuscript a hundred times since he had first hacked it out on a worn electric typewriter over twenty years ago during his senior year of high school. The two hundred pages comprised what he more or less referred to as his first novel, though it had never been published. It was a horror novel entitled *Blue Moon*, the story of a teenage boy cursed with lycanthropy and his flight from his hometown when as a werewolf he kills the girl he loves. But during the last couple of months he had dug this same raggedy manila envelope from his dusty pile of good intentions and half-planned ideas to see if it could be salvaged, and after a couple of weeks staring at it he would hide it away again. The idea was there but it lacked structure, and as many times as he read over it there didn't seem to be a way to redeem it.

While in college, majoring in English and washing dishes in a grimy truck stop restaurant to help pay for it, he tried half-heartedly and unsuccessfully to sell *Blue Moon*, his hopes rising fervently each time he sent it off to New York, only to have them dashed when his manuscript came back with a standard rejection slip. Finally after a year he stopped mailing it out.

Then, in his third year at the university he met Katherine ("Call me 'Kat,'" she told him). She was a freshman, also majoring in English, and he saw her at the library often. Sometimes she sat in the quad with a spiral notebook, writing – poems, he later discovered. Like Lee, she had lost her father during her teens; they discussed that during their first conversation, just like old friends. Soon they were talking about books ("I *hate* romance novels," she said), and then he was walking her to her dorm, and suddenly they were going out on weekends, talking about love and sex and possibly marriage.

"I don't want to," he could hear her saying, her voice as sharp and clear as it had been that night in his room all those years ago. Steve, his roommate, had gone to a James Dean film festival at the student center, leaving the two of them alone for the first time in weeks. They had just polished off a pizza and a bottle of wine, and things had been going fine on Lee's bed until he had started unbuttoning her blouse. She grabbed his hand immediately. "No. I don't want to."

He crawled off the bed and sat sullen on the floor, his erection throbbing and his lips red and numb from kissing, while she lay on the bed buttoning her blouse. "Sorry," she said. "I'm just not ready yet. I know you probably think that's stupid. . . "

"It's all right," he told her. "We'll have plenty of time for that. I'll always respect you, Kat."

Her rejection made him love her more, and when she finally did give in one wet December evening during finals week, it was as wonderful and beautiful as he had imagined. Being in love with Kat filled him with inspiration and hope. He wrote every moment he had a chance. Kat encouraged him, crying at his maudlin short stories and urging him to send them to small literary magazines. When a quarterly out of Minnesota published him the fall of his senior year, he and Kat walked on air for weeks. Kat published a few poems herself, and while Lee felt they were more stylish than heartfelt, he couldn't help but be proud of her. Lee saw the two of them growing old together, he successfully writing novel after novel while she churned out acclaimed poetry.

Then came graduation. And grad school. Lee pushed himself and earned his master's within a year, and then he was offered a job teaching freshman comp at a private college in Cedar Hill, two hundred miles away. "I can't take it," he told Kat. "You can't finish school there, and I can't leave you behind."

"You've got to take it," she said.

"I can't do it, babe. I can't go all the way out there without you."

"You have to," she told him. "We can see each other on weekends. It's not that far."

So he took it, and for several months he made the drive back and forth, spending weekends at her place. Usually both her roommates were gone and it was just the two of them, and he liked pretending they were married and living in their own little apartment. Sunday afternoons were rough, and he hated the gnawing in his gut that accompanied him all the way back to Cedar Hill. He and Kat would talk on the phone several times during the week, but gradually he could no longer lie to himself that she wasn't becoming distant; they hadn't made love in several weeks, and most of their time together anymore was spent arguing. In the end, they were forced to acknowledge that the relationship was not working and they decided to end it. She moved to the west coast and he stayed cooped up in Cedar Hill.

When Kat was out of his life, Lee began to write again in earnest. Several more stories were picked up by small literaries, and he started work on a new novel. Weekends were empty now; he had no desire to date anyone yet, so most nights and weekends were spent sitting in front of his computer, staring at a blank screen and drinking pots of black coffee.

His second year at Cedar Hill he was offered a creative writing class that met on Wednesday nights, and while that ate into his writing time, he was glad to be discussing more sophisticated writing topics than comparison/contrast papers. While he had never considered himself a literary genius, he was surprised at the awkwardness of most of his students' work. Most of it was truly awful – rhyming stanzas about flowers and kids, rambling stories about unrequited love and the occasional Stephen King horror rip-off.

So when the simple beauty of a character sketch by a student named Jessica Winters came across his desk one late October night, Lee took great notice. The assignment had been to create a character who was mourning a loss – anything was game. Amid the messily-typed and badly punctuated outlines of little girls crying over kittens and teenage boys losing fathers came a gem about an old man who had lost his family's farm to foreclosure. He read it twice, then set it aside and read it again when he had finished all the others.

After the class met the next time, Lee asked her to

remain afterwards to discuss her paper. "It's about my grandfather," she told him. "He lost his farm during the recession in the early eighties. I remember watching him while they auctioned off his equipment. He just sat on the edge of the front porch and stared out across the fields, like he was looking at something I couldn't see. He died just a few months afterward. It was like he had nothing to live for after that."

Against his better judgment and totally outside of his character, he asked her to join him for coffee at the shop down the street. To his delight she accepted, and they spent the next three hours talking about everything imaginable. She was a junior from upstate attending on a full-ride scholarship, majoring in broadcast journalism but unsure of what she wanted to do with her life. "I don't want to work for some crumby small-town TV station," she sneered. "I know how those places operate. I'd be stuck doing fluff pieces about kids and dogs. I want to do serious journalism – something that will make a difference."

Lee both admired her passion and was intimidated by it. There was no doubt she was driven, and that excited him. Kat had been talented, but her work and her personality lacked fire. Jessica – or Jessie as she asked him to call her – had it. After that first evening, he thought about her every day, but out of a moral obligation he didn't ask her out again until the semester ended. She gave him the number at her mother's house where she would be over the holidays and told him to call her. They talked often over Christmas break, and after returning to the college they were together almost every night.

A little over a year later, they were married in a

simple ceremony at Jessie's home church. After a brief honeymoon in the mountains, they returned to Cedar Hill to settle into a routine of teaching and school. By the time Jessie graduated, she was nine months pregnant with Lizbeth. "We're going to need a bigger place," she told Lee. Though she was tempted to accept an offer with the local newspaper, she ultimately refused. "I'm going to stay home with this baby if it kills me and you both."

They found a stone cottage within walking distance of the college and fell in love with it immediately, even though it was a crumbling mess. "A fireplace!" he said to her. "We have our very own fireplace!" They fixed the place up as cozily as they could on their tight budget, trying carefully to plan for the added expense of the baby.

And suddenly Lizbeth was in their lives. It was a huge change, but Lee thought he adjusted well. He was up early in the mornings and off for his first class at eight, then back home by five or six. After dinner, when he wasn't helping Jessie, looking over student work or teaching a night class, he wrote. He had written a few short stories, but now he felt the need to work on a book again. He just couldn't say all he wanted in a short story. It was slow-going at first; after all, he hadn't worked on this scale for about six years. Constant interruptions by the baby made it difficult for him to stay in the mood at times, and some nights he simply gave up after slaving through only a page or so.

After a year and a half the novel was finished, though he knew it wasn't very good. Still, he sent it off to New York with vague hopes, and it was returned promptly with one handwritten word scrawled across the top of his cover letter: "Sorry." He ripped the note and the manuscript to shreds and burned it all in the fireplace, then downed half a pint of Maker's Mark and passed out after a failed attempt to make love to Jessie.

Over the next few days he wallowed in self-pity and embarrassment at his outburst.

"Just send it back out to some other place," Jessie told him.

"No, I'm not sending it off anymore. They're right, it's terrible."

"I liked it."

"Oh, Jessie." He kissed her hand. "If I wrote a grocery list, you'd like it."

"Are you going to start something else then?"

"I don't know. Maybe. I just don't want to spend the rest of my life teaching freshman English and reading scores of horrible three-point themes."

He did not write anything for several years. By that time, Corey had been born and Lee had moved up to teaching American literature. While teaching, he realized he was once again falling in love with the form of the novel, though he did not want to. "I don't want to write anymore," he told Jessie one night as they lay in the darkness of their bedroom. "I don't want to work and work on something that's just going to be rejected. It's pointless."

"Why don't you work on some more short stories?"

"I don't know. The market's pretty well dried up for that now. And those literary magazines don't pay in anything but copies these days. What the hell are we gonna do with five copies of *Ploughshares*?"

"Well, you've got to stay in practice," she said. "You can't think about rejection or payment or markets.

You can't think about anything but what you're writing, and you can't write for anyone but yourself."

He looked at her. "You'd've made a good writer, Jess."

The next day Lee didn't go in for his classes; instead, spurred on by some capricious inspiration he fired up his PC and churned out twenty pages of a new story. He wrote furiously, not stopping to rest or eat, completely oblivious to anything around him. He staggered to bed at midnight, exhausted. The day after, he went to class but started writing as soon as he returned home. And he wrote the next day and the next and the next. In a little over a month he completed his third novel.

He called it *Max Plexico and the Vault of Osiris*, and though the manuscript barely covered two hundred pages, it was easy to see that it was the best work he had ever done. The story concerned twelve-year-old adventurer Max Plexico investigating a looted tomb and evading a band of mercenaries intent on using his discovery for world domination. It was steampunk juvenile fiction, set in an alternate reality, a genre he had never considered before.

"Why a children's book?" Jessie asked after she finished it. "I mean, it's excellent, but where did that come from?"

"I don't know," Lee told her. "I saw a picture in an old issue of National Geographic one day on a desk in the library - a young boy wearing an aviator's cap with goggles and standing in front of the pyramids. For some reason it just stayed with me." He looked at her. "I think this could be something, Jess. Something big. I could write a whole series of books about this character."

With newfound enthusiasm but not really expecting much, Lee sent off three sample chapters to one of the largest publishing houses in New York. For four long months he heard nothing. "It must have been lost in the mail," he told Jessie.

"Maybe you should write them and see if they got it," she suggested. "It couldn't hurt anything."

Then one morning, while he sat at the kitchen table downing black coffee in an attempt to undo all the bourbon from the previous night, Jessie floated into the room, her face drained of color. He stared at her, his heart thudding in his ears. "Jess. . . What is it?"

She held up a cream-colored envelope. "It's a letter. From them."

He could faintly see CIRCLE PUBLISHING emblazoned on the back. "I'm sure it's just a rejection letter," he said. "You—you read it, Jessie. I just can't."

She tore open the envelope and read the message inside, her face expressionless. Suddenly, she gasped. "They like it," she cried. "They want to see more!"

Lee gathered the remaining chapters and mailed them off the next morning. For six weeks the two of them barely spoke, barely looked at each other, barely moved as if they were walking barefoot on crushed glass.

Then Corey became ill with pneumonia. Lee and Jessie took turns alternating between the hospital and staying home with Lizbeth. For six long, long days they hardly slept or ate. But Corey was strong, and soon he was back home.

"What are we gonna do, Lee?" Jessie asked one Saturday morning after a late breakfast. "We've got so many bills. Have you seen the statement from the hospital for Corey? How are we gonna pay that? The car insurance is due next month and—"

"I know, I know," he said, waving a hand at her. "I don't know what to do. I could go to Mom, I guess, but I think she's worse off than we are." He looked at her. "What about your family?"

She frowned. "We've gone to my mother so much, I'm ashamed to ask her for anything else."

"What if we got a bill consolidation loan?"

"I don't know…"

Lee pounded his fist on the table. "God, I hate this. I hate living this way. I feel like I've failed in everything I've ever done. When I asked you to marry me, I never thought we'd be living on the edge of poverty."

"Don't be so dramatic," Jessie said. "I don't think we're quite seeing poverty."

"I just feel like you and the kids deserve a lot better than this. I want to—"

"Somebody's at the door," Jessie interrupted, holding up her hand.

"I don't hear anything."

"Somebody knocked."

Lee pushed himself back from the table, sighing. "Probably a bill collector." He made his way into the living room, pausing to turn down the blaring television as Lizbeth was opening the front door.

The mailman was waiting on the stoop, his Jeep rumbling out in the street. "Got a registered letter for ya." He held out a small clipboard in his large pudgy hand. "Sign here, please. Number twelve."

Lee scrawled his name on the line and handed the board back to the mailman. He was vaguely aware that

Corey was crawling between his feet. He stooped to pick up the boy and grabbed the letter at the same time.

The mailman glanced at the signature. "Thanks, have a good day."

Jessie appeared in the room as Lee closed the door. "Who was it?"

"Daddy got a western letter," Lizbeth chirped.

"Registered," Lee corrected her.

"Who's it from?"

He looked at the envelope. "Oh, my God."

"What is it? Is it from the hospital? Are they filing suit?"

"Oh, God, it's from the publisher."

"Oh, my God." She took Corey from his arms. "Open it, open it!"

He ripped into the letter and read it hastily, then read it again. "Oh, my God." He sank to his knees, then flopped to the floor on his buttocks.

"What in God's name do they say!"

He looked up at her. "They took it. They took the book. They want a whole series. They're advancing me fifteen thousand dollars."

Jessie's mouth dropped open. "Holy shit!"

Behind them, Lizbeth began to giggle. "You look funny, Daddy."

● ● ●

Lee's glass was dry.

He pushed his chair back from the desk and glanced through the panes of the French doors. The den was dark and quiet. His watch said ten-thirty; presumably, Jessie and Lizbeth had already headed up to bed. He had been in here daydreaming for an hour and a half.

He swung his chair around and his gaze fell on the nearest bookshelf – the shelf stuffed with his books.

Actually, it was Max Plexico's shelf. All twelve books in the series, several editions of each. The British versions. The French versions. The German versions. Hell, even the Japanese versions with the anime-style illustrations. Then there were the movie tie-in paperback editions for the first three books, each emblazoned with the Max Plexico logo and the movie poster art. And standing guard over the books, a Max Plexico action figure – one of the first – given to him by Mattel. It was Max's shelf, all right. Everything around him – the books, the house, his land – all of it was Max's.

He pulled down the leather-bound collector's edition of *Max Plexico and the Vault of Osiris* and ran his fingertips over the gilded letters, the stylized "MP" logo on the front cover, then began to leaf through it. It really was a handsome book, from the heavy cotton-blend pages to the delicate watercolor illustrations throughout. It was everything he'd ever imagined about holding a copy of his own work. For comparison, he shelved it and pulled out the paperback movie tie in whose cover was emblazoned with the face of Justin Alexander, the teen actor who played Max in the three movies. He was dressed to the hilt in adventure gear and looked more as if he were ready to fight off a mob of schoolgirls than explore an ancient tomb.

Lee had actually met Justin Alexander in August while visiting the shoot of the fourth movie in New Mexico. Justin Alexander was a spoiled twit, a fourteen-year-old who had every production assistant on the set walking on eggshells around him. He screamed after every take that he needed his bottle of Evian, and it had better be cold this time or someone would get their ass chewed out, and where were his goddamn sunglasses because Jesus Christ it was bright out here and fucking hot and he was going back to his trailer to cool down. Lee left the set disillusioned and stunned, and he vowed to never visit a production again.

He placed the paperback on the shelf and switched off the lamps in the study. He had spent too much time brooding today. Hopefully tomorrow would be better.

Jessie's light was out when he went upstairs. "Good night," he called to her as he passed, but there was no response and he was sure she was already asleep. He felt a slight sting tempered only by the fact that things had been this way between them for a while now. Their communication was strained but polite, more like the interaction of two acquaintances rather than husband and wife. They rarely touched these days, and her hand on his shoulder on the porch tonight was the closest thing to intimacy they'd experienced in months. They began drifting apart about the time the second Max Plexico book was published, when Lee was just starting to feel panicky about his future as a writer, when he started questioning how he was going to follow up a series of wildly successful children's books and which direction his career should take. Jessie responded to his moodiness by accepting a job as a local morning television news anchor and throwing herself into her work. "I want to actually do something with my degree," she told him, although they both knew that was her excuse to get out of the house and begin building her own life. A life that was looking more and more these days as if it didn't include him.

He'd begun sleeping in the guestroom sometime a couple of years back. And while the official reason had to do with Jessie's crazy schedule and leaving for work in the middle of the night, there was a sense of relief that they no longer had to keep up the appearance of being lovers. Jessie was already gone in the mornings when he arose and she was usually in bed at seven, even on the weekends. When the kids weren't in school that left very little time for the two of them to be alone, for which Jessie seemed grateful.

In the guestroom he brushed his teeth in the small attached bath, then slipped out of his clothes and under the covers. The sheets were cold, and he balled himself up until the heat of his body had warmed the bed. He picked up his iPad to read for a while, but then set it aside and switched off his lamp. His mind felt fuzzy and tired, and he didn't feel like spending his waning energy trying to concentrate on a story.

As usual, he had accomplished nothing today. Besides thumbing once again through the old manuscript, he sorted through his old college papers, checked email. Played on Facebook and Goodreads. Mostly sat at the desk and thought. He hadn't even managed to get in his workout. The thought of actually sitting down and putting new words on paper was crushing. He had read an article not long ago on burnout, and the description of symptoms hit uncomfortably close to home. He wanted to do nothing – to write nothing, to read nothing, to think nothing. So far he was at least accomplishing that.

But he couldn't afford to *do* nothing. Bill Cosgrove, his agent in New York, was expecting an outline on something within the next week. Bill had been with Lee since the sale of the first book eight years ago, and Lee didn't want to do anything that might jeopardize the trust Bill had in him. Up to now Bill had been extremely patient, as had the folks at Circle, and Lee couldn't put them off any longer. But he still had no idea what he was going to send to Bill. No idea at all. He still wasn't even sure which direction he wanted to go – whether he wanted to stick with children's fiction or branch out to something more grown-up. As for Circle, Bill claimed they didn't care, that he was at a point in his career where he could do what he wanted for the three books under the new contract. He just had to figure out what it was he actually wanted.

Maybe he needed a change of scenery. There was the cabin over at Harper's Lake. What if he went out there by himself for just a few weeks? If he took his clothes and his laptop, stocked up on enough food and coffee to get him through until spring and had nothing to distract him, he just might be able to pull it off. He had even told Jessie once back last summer that the lake was inspiring, and that someday he'd have to stay out there and get some writing done. Maybe that time was now. Tomorrow was Friday. Perhaps he would load everything up and go on out there this weekend. He could be writing as early as Saturday afternoon.

While he was at it, maybe he would drive on over to the college at Cedar Hill and take Corey's fireflies to the science department. Surely someone there could shed some light on why fireflies would suddenly swarm up in the dead of winter. Maybe he had some special genetic mutation of firefly, or perhaps a different species had drifted in from somewhere else. The whole thing was odd, and he would sure be happy for someone with some expertise to have a look at them.

But in the morning, the fireflies in Corey's jar had disappeared.

* * *

"Where are they, Daddy?"

Lee stared at the jar. The lid was still closed as tightly as it had been last night, yet the fireflies were gone. Completely vanished. "Did you let them out? I know you were watching them right before you went to sleep last night."

"No," he said. And the hurt expression in his eyes told Lee he was being truthful. "Did they run away?"

Lee frowned. "Fireflies don't run away. Not out of a sealed jar." He looked at the tiny holes he'd made in the lid with an icepick. No way they escaped through there. "I don't get it."

Lizbeth stuck her head in the doorway. Her hair was frizzy and her eyes were puffy with sleep. "What's going on?"

Lee held up the empty jar. "They're gone."

Lizbeth's eyes widened. "What?" She took the jar from him and peered inside, turning it over in her hands. "How?"

"That's what I'd like to know," Lee said.

Lizbeth glanced at Corey with her eyes narrowed. "Corey, did you – "

"No!" Corey said. "Dad already asked me that."

Lee took the jar from Lizbeth and stared at it. It was completely empty. Not a cast-off wing or a speck of dirt. It was as if they had never existed.

Fireflies are sometimes seen as one of the portents

of death.

He shuddered and ruffled Corey's hair. "Let's all get breakfast so I can get you two to school." They took one last look at the empty jar. "I just don't get it," Lee said.

* * *

As usual, the traffic around the school was heavy and chaotic. Moms in a hurry to get their precious kids unloaded and get to work; dads fresh off an eight-hour third shift, cranky and tired and in no mood for traffic niceties. Then there were the buses disgorging a sea of elementary kids and the occasional child on foot weaving his way through the line of cars like a live action version of Frogger. Added to that was a cold mix of light rain and sleet that had begun to fall and the mind-numbing *thump-thump* of the wipers across the windshield. Nothing filled Lee with road rage more than circling the drive around East Madison Elementary.

"You've got the permission slip for Mrs. Dixon about the field trip to the science center next week, right Lizbeth?"

Lizbeth rolled her eyes. "Yes, Dad. And I've got the five dollars that goes with it."

"Good girl." Lee glanced at Corey in the rearview mirror. "You picked up your library book off the table before we left, didn't you?"

"In my backpack," Corey announced.

"Today's library day," Lee reminded him. "If you don't have your book – "

"Dad," Lizabeth said, placing a mittened hand on Lee's arm, "he's got it."

Lee nodded, giving her a terse smile. "Just

checking."

The car inched through the traffic, moving closer to the drop-off point. They had almost reached the covered sidewalk when he spotted her – Kat. She was hurrying a small girl through the rain toward the front door of the school, both of them wearing red wool coats and huddled beneath a large pink umbrella. For a moment, all Lee could do was stare, letting the tidal wave of emotions wash over him – anger, hurt, love. Then the woman turned toward him and he saw with sadness and surprise that it *wasn't* Kat. But the resemblance was uncanny. She had the same honey-colored hair and dark eyes, the same cool, composed demeanor. In recent years he had begun searching for Kat on the internet every so often, just out of curiosity but he'd never found much. When her first book of poetry was published a few years ago, he had bought a copy, though he kept it hidden down at the lake house. He had not wanted Jessie to get the wrong idea. He by no means ever wished for a life with Kat instead of Jessie, but seeing her lookalike now there was no denying the aching scar Kat's departure had left on him.

Lee pulled to a stop at the school entrance, watching as Kat's twin and her daughter disappeared through the double doors into the warmly-lit foyer. A daughter. It was hard to imagine Kat with a daughter. The biography on her book's jacket was infuriatingly vague, saying only that she was married and lived in the Pacific Northwest. He wondered if Kat had ever had children.

Lizbeth and Corey popped open the doors of the Escalade and stepped out into the rain. "'Bye, Dad," Corey said.

"'Bye, kiddos."

Lizbeth started to close her door but stopped, eyeing Lee. "You okay, Dad?"

"Fine," Lee said. "Go on, don't be late."

She continued to look at him as she shut the door, and he felt a sense of relief when she finally turned and made her way to the front door of the school. He hadn't realized his feelings for Kat had shown so plainly on his face. He took a deep breath. He needed to get back home and get his mind on something else. Quickly.

Behind him, a horn honked impatiently, and Lee lifted his hand in an apologetic wave. The horn sounded again. "Yeah, fuck you, too, buddy," he muttered.

* * *

By the time Jessie got home with the kids after school, Lee had made arrangements for Lizbeth and Corey. He'd also called for the internet and satellite TV to be turned back on at the cabin and for a load of firewood to be delivered. If he was going to hole himself up at the lake, he wanted to make sure he was warm and cozy and plenty entertained. He'd debated about having the satellite TV reconnected; after all, the whole purpose of this venture was for him to be undisturbed so he could write. But going without news and weather reports for three months seemed incomprehensible. And while the cabin was equipped with central heat, it would be foolish to winter there without a secondary source of heat should the power go out.

He was in the middle of packing his winter clothes when Jessie appeared at the doorway of the guest room. "What are you doing? You going somewhere?" Her face wore a mere inquisitive expression, but there was no covering the hint of panic in her voice. It was sad really, and for the first time in months Lee actually felt something akin to affection for her.

He pulled a sweater from the dresser drawer and placed it in the suitcase. "Remember when we talked about me going down to the lake house to write? I've decided it's time."

"Now?"

He looked at her. "Why not?"

She sank onto the bed. "I just. . . never expected you'd actually do it. And why there? You know I hate that place."

"Look," he said, "I've got to get something done. I've fucked around for months without writing a single word. I need a change, Jessie. I need to get away from everything here and be by myself for a while. Just to think. To concentrate. With no distractions."

Jessie picked at a loose thread on the bedspread. "I thought you were doing a pretty good job avoiding distractions by shutting yourself up in that office every day."

"You know what I mean."

"No," she said. "I *don't* know what you mean. Am I a distraction to you? Are Lizbeth and Corey just *distractions*?"

He took a deep breath. He'd been afraid of this, of her overreacting. "That's not what I'm saying at all. But. . . yes, in a way you're all distracting me from getting anything done. I need quiet and solitude."

Jessie sniffed and Lee realized she was holding back tears. "How long will you be gone?"

"I don't know yet. Probably until spring."

She shot him a look. "*Spring*? You're going to leave us alone until spring?"

"It's only a couple of months, Jessie."

She shook her head and went back to picking at the loose thread. "Have you told them yet?"

"Not yet. I figured we'd tell them together."

"And how do you suggest we do that?" she spat. "Sit them down to a nice dinner and say, 'Oh by the way, your father's leaving'?" She gave a loud sigh.

"It's not like they'll never see me again," Lee said, feeling irritation burn in his chest. "It's not like we're getting divorced."

Jessie looked at him. "Are you sure? Are you sure this isn't just the first step toward splitting up for good?"

He had picked up a Cedar Hill College sweatshirt and froze just before placing it in the suitcase. "To be honest, I don't know." He laid the sweatshirt atop the sweater and looked at her. "Is that what you want?"

She held his gaze for a moment, then looked back at the loose thread. "I don't know."

"Neither do I." He stepped toward her and placed his hands on her shoulders. "I *need* this Jessie. I need this time to myself."

She nodded and the first tears spilled down her cheeks. She brushed them away with her fingertips. "I know you do." She patted his arm. "You should do this. Really."

He looked at her once more, feeling something give a little in his chest, and turned back to his packing. "I've made arrangements with Cindy Martin to take the kids to school each day. You can pick them up in the afternoon as always."

She glanced up. "What about the mornings? I won't be here to get them up and fed and dressed. I'll already be at work. And you know Lizbeth still can't fix her own hair."

"I talked to your mother," Lee said, his eyes fixed on the clothes folded in the suitcase. "She said she could come stay as long as we needed her to."

"You called *Mom*?" She sat back and blew out a breath. "I guess you've thought of everything then."

"I tried."

"Did it occur to you to even consider consulting me before you made all these plans?"

He eased down onto the bed beside her. "We both know when we start hashing things out, nothing gets done. We would have hemmed and hawed over the details until Lizbeth was in college." He grabbed her hands. "Jessie, if I don't do this now, I'll never do it at all. I've got to turn in an outline of something by the end of next week. I've got to get my ass in gear. I can't afford to put Bill off any longer."

She nodded. "I know you're right."

He gave her a smile. "If it's any consolation, your mom is really excited about staying here for a couple of months."

Jessie rolled her eyes. "I bet she is."

"It could be worse," Lee said. "It could be *my* mother."

In spite of her tears, Jessie laughed.

* * *

Saturday morning dawned bright and warm. The wintry ice and rain of Friday had given way to a blue cloudless sky, and a balmy breeze from the south made the day spring-like. The warmth of the sun on his face gave Lee hope, and for the first time in months he felt invigorated and alive.

Lee and Jessie barely spoke as the Escalade was loaded with Lee's belongings. Neither looked the other in the eye, as if by acknowledging the other's existence a flood of emotion would be unleashed. Corey helped, packing Lee's well-worn thesaurus and a shopping bag full of highlighters and pens. Lizbeth remained silent in her room, even when Lee knocked softly on her door to tell her he was leaving; some sort of punishment for him, he supposed.

Just as he pulled out of the drive, he caught sight of Corey standing in the front door, his blond hair shimmering in the sunlight. Beside him sat the gray cat. Corey raised his hand and waved. His face was forlorn and wet with tears. Lee waved back, trying to ignore the ball of hurt that suddenly appeared in his throat. He and Corey looked at each other for a moment, and then Lee drove away. In the rearview mirror, he could see Corey watching him until the car rounded the bend and thankfully the house disappeared from view.

The drive from Springfield to Harper's Lake took about an hour. The flat, wide interstate gave way to a two-lane road that wound through hills and pine forest before descending into the lakeside village. Although this was off-season, the town was bustling with locals doing their Saturday errands, and the narrow streets were thick with traffic.

The hardware store seemed to be doing a booming business, and several men that looked to range in age from their late teens to their seventies milled about in front, some in Carhartt bibs, some in denim overalls, all of them in animated conversation. He envied them. They were content with their small-town lives, happy to go to work each day in factories or offices or on farms and come home to their wives and families and kick back with a beer or two in front of the TV. They weren't cursed with the need to create, to write. They weren't plagued with the constant flow of thoughts and ideas and the incessant self-doubt that came with them. They were unburdened by the notion that there might be something bigger outside the lake valley. There was something to be said for not having an inflated sense of self-importance, but much as he had tried, Lee had never been able to dispose of his.

Even with the pills and the endless sessions with Dr. Thayer.

He'd first sought out therapy last summer, hoping discussing his fears and disappointments with a disinterested third party would help his writer's block. Instead, Dr. Thayer had prescribed anti-depressants and asked him pointless questions about his childhood, his relationship with his parents, his sex life with Jessie. The sessions were fruitless, and the pills only served to dull his mind and make writing that much more difficult. Just before Christmas he had stopped the visits to Dr. Thayer and had flushed the remaining pills down the toilet. He never told Jessie about the therapy and drugs, and she never asked.

He pulled into the crowded lot of the main grocery in town and made his way down the aisles, filling his cart with canned items and frozen dinners, enough to last him at least a month, then piled them into the back of the Escalade with all his other bags. But just as he hit the top of the hill outside of town, he remembered he'd forgotten coffee. And God knew there would be no writing without coffee. But no matter. There was a small general store just before the turnoff to the cabin, and he was pretty sure they would carry coffee.

He turned off the pavement, the Escalade's tires crunching on the gravel lot, and pulled up to the white clapboard structure. Inside he threaded his way through the maze of racks displaying sunglasses and snack cakes, past the dazzling lottery kiosks and found the coffee. Wow. Convenience store prices were outrageous.

"Can I help you?" Lee looked up to see a portly grizzled man in a red flannel shirt emerge from an open doorway behind the counter. Old Mr. Saunders. He'd owned this place for years.

"Just grabbing some coffee," Lee said, bringing the container up to the register.

Mr. Saunders squinted at him. "You're that writer fella, aren't you?"

"Yes, afraid so."

Mr. Saunders snapped his fingers and pointed at him. "Houston. Lee Houston. You all have that nice big place on the north end of the lake."

Lee nodded. "That's me."

"Haven't seen you in here since last summer. Our granddaughter was here over Christmas. She was reading one of your books. Got real excited when I told her you guys had a house out here." He smiled, showing tobacco-stained teeth.

"How old is she?"

"She's twelve. Always got a book in her hands."

Lee felt a sting of hurt in his chest. Same age as Lizbeth. Lizbeth who had refused to acknowledge his departure this morning. "My daughter reads a lot, too."

Mr. Saunders took the coffee and rang it up. "So what brings you out here this time of year?"

"Working on a project," Lee said. "Gonna spend the winter out here and try to finish it up." He slid a twenty across the counter. "Need some peace and quiet."

Mr. Saunders slammed the register closed and handed Lee his change. "Your family come out with you?"

"No," Lee said. "They stayed back in Springfield. The kids have school and Jessie's job – "

"You mean you'll be out here all by yourself?"

"That's the plan."

Mr. Saunders leaned closer. "You be careful."

Lee straightened. "I will."

"You got a good alarm system on that house?"

Lee felt a spark of irritation. "Certainly do."

"Don't mean to scare you," Mr. Saunders said, scratching the silver stubble under his chin, "but hoodlums have been known to take advantage of this time of year to break into these lake houses. Especially the nicer ones. You see anybody lurking around out there that shouldn't be, you call the sheriff pronto."

"We've never had any problems in the five years we've owned our place."

Mr. Saunders nodded. "Good. Let's hope it stays that way." He lowered his voice, as if unseen customers might overhear. "Last winter somebody broke into the Millers' house right next to yours."

"The A-frame?"

"Yep. Killed a cat in there. Wrote things all over the walls with its blood. Terrible things. Cut off the poor thing's head and impaled it on a pole. Left the pole sticking in the ground right by the front door."

Lee's stomach clenched in revulsion. "Jesus Christ."

"David and Linda's little boy found it first. He was traumatized."

Lee had seen the Millers in passing. Their son Thomas was younger than Corey. "Did they figure out who did it?"

"No." Mr. Saunders sat back on a stool and crossed his arms. "Sheriff said he thought it might be some kind of cult. There was a pentagram drawn on the floor. Also in blood."

"Cat's blood?"

"Human. Never found out whose."

Lee swallowed and looked away, grabbing the canister of coffee. "Well, I'd love to stay and chat, but I really need to get going."

"Sure, sure," Mr. Saunders said. "Listen, you get too lonely, you come up and visit me and Gracie." He pointed to a neat, well-kept farmhouse across the road. "We live just over there. Love to have you for dinner sometime. Gracie cooks a mean pot roast."

"Thanks," Lee said. "But I doubt I'll get too lonely. I'm looking forward to spending some time by myself with no interruptions or distractions."

"You know, bein' alone out here ain't like bein' alone in the city. Particularly this time of year. Only two or three of these houses are occupied in the winter. Only the die-hards stay on past the summer. I won't kid you. It gets rough out here. Especially when the snow hits and you're stuck inside. Especially when you're by yourself. Been known to drive a man crazy."

"Yeah," Lee said, "cabin fever. I'll be all right. I – "

"You got a gun, Mr. Houston?"

Lee stared at him. There was no gun in the house. He'd never liked guns, and he certainly didn't want one while the kids were still small. But there was no way he was telling that to this old buzzard. "Yeah," Lee lied. "Yeah. I have a Glock."

Mr. Saunders nodded. "Keep it loaded. And handy."

"I will."

"Remember, if you have trouble out here, it'll take the sheriff a good twenty minutes to reach you from town. And that's if the roads are clear. They don't plow these lake roads in the winter, so if you hear of a big snowstorm headed this way, you be sure and lay you in some supplies. And if the power goes out down there, you're on your own. Could be days before it's fixed. Make sure you got a way to keep warm."

"Got a load of firewood coming," Lee said. He was beginning to feel irritated. After all, he was almost forty, not fourteen. He did know things.

"Good," Mr. Saunders said. "You stay safe down there. And I meant what I said about coming to visit. Gracie and I don't get much company in the winter."

Lee nodded and headed toward the door. "Take care, Mr. Saunders."

Outside, he climbed into the Escalade and sat looking at the road where the turnoff disappeared down a hill into a grove of tall pines. The conversation with Mr. Saunders had left him uneasy with all that talk about prowlers and cults and dead cats. He started the engine and pulled out of the parking lot toward the road to the cabin, shaking his head. He had to get hold of himself if he was going to be alone for two months.

● ● ●

The narrow paved road wound through the woods toward the water, and the carpet of yellowed pine needles on the forest floor still held on to patches of snow from the previous day where the weak winter sunlight couldn't reach. Even this time of the year when most everything else was dead and brown, the drive down to the cabin through the towering pines was still beautiful. He rounded a bend and caught sight of the water shimmering through the trees, steely gray and agitated, and he felt a chill ripple through him. The outside temperature on the dash read forty-five, and he'd doffed his jacket just outside of Springfield. But the glint of the sun across the lake stabbed at his eyes like needles, and he shivered in spite of the warmth of the Escalade.

The gravel drive to the cabin appeared just beyond a stand of bare locust trees and snaked its way toward the green metal roof of the cabin. He turned off the pavement and coasted down the slight slope beneath the arch of intertwined oak limbs, and the house and lake loomed into view.

The cabin was two-story structure constructed of interlocking logs, stained redwood planks, and river rock – a blend of rustic, contemporary, and farm cottage. They'd purchased it five years ago when the film rights to the first Max Plexico book had sold. Jessie had wanted a summer getaway, and when the house on Harper's Lake came up for sale they'd gone to look at it. Lee immediately fell in love. It was everything their sprawling house in Springfield was not. Unpretentious, outdated, and surrounded by nature.

Jessie hated it at first. Hated it even more after they bought it and discovered an infestation of termites which was expensively remedied. She hated the lake, especially in the summer when early morning fishing boats were puttering across the water while she was trying to sleep in. She was terrified Corey would wander off from the house and they'd find him floating face-down next to the dock, a fear that never seemed to abate even as Corey grew older and more responsible. She begrudgingly accompanied Lee and the kids on trips out here, but she always drove separately so she could leave early to "go take care of things at home." More than anything, she seemed to loathe the idea of calling it a "cabin," as if she were being forced to haul water from a stream and prepare meals over an open fire. After a couple of summers, Lee realized that Jessie resented spending her time with ordinary people when she could be hobnobbing with the upper crust in Springfield at affairs they ostentatiously called "barbecues" and "teas." Jessie was a city girl, and the casual middle-class atmosphere of Harper's Lake was beneath her. It should have been his first warning, he thought.

He turned off the engine and sat in the silence for a moment, looking over the outside of the house. Mr. Saunders' warnings and the grisly story of the Millers' vandalism flashed through his mind, and he found himself wishing he really did have a Glock concealed somewhere inside.

He climbed out of the Escalade and rounded the cabin, looking for any tell-tale signs of forced entry. Everything seemed secure. No cracked windows or busted doorframes. Not so much as a lawn chair out of place. He was pleased to see the firewood had already been delivered and was neatly stacked in the lean-to next to the house.

He climbed up the steps to the back deck and gazed out over the lake. Way on the other side he could barely make out the town huddled beneath a haze of wood smoke and the occasional flash of the sun glinting off a car's windows. The breeze whipping off the water was sharp, and he cursed himself for leaving his jacket in the SUV. The crisp air smelled of dried leaves with only a faint fishy smell from the lake.

The quiet. It was nearly deafening. No boats on the lake. No traffic on the lane. No birds singing. No leaves on the trees to rustle in the wind. It was as if he'd entered a cocoon, a place where nothing else could reach him. Nothing could disturb him. Nothing could distract him. If he couldn't write here, he was doomed.

He dug out his phone and fired off a quick text to Jessie: *I'm here.*

While he waited for her to respond he peered down the slope to the water and the dock. A trail led along the lake's edge. He and the kids had followed it back in the summer until Lizbeth tired out and pleaded to go back to the cabin. It probably went for miles. Tomorrow he might check it out. And this time he could walk as far as he damned well pleased.

His phone vibrated and he glanced at the reply from Jessie: *Ok.*

He wrote back, *It's beautiful here!*

He waited for her to text back, but after a few minutes he realized she wasn't going to. Well, fuck her anyway. He shoved the phone back in his pocket and headed toward the front of the house. He needed to get unpacked and settled.

* * *

Inside, the house was cold and musty. Lee carried the groceries through the living room with its log walls and well-worn furniture to the kitchen, which had probably seen its last remodel some time in the 'nineties. Jessie always hated this kitchen, hated its mud-colored laminate countertops and rustic wooden cabinets, its white appliances and dated cast-iron sink. Well, she wasn't here now, which was just fine with him. There would be no one to complain or nag or respond to his comments with only a grunt or disinterested "Hhmm." He set the bags down and looked about with a contented sigh, savoring the quiet.

Through the patio doors across the dining room he could see the lake beyond the deck. Even though he couldn't feel the wind in here, he still felt a chill. That gray water...constantly moving, constantly agitated. Cold. Lifeless. Yet...not dead.

He shivered. Heat. That's what he needed.

The thermostat was set to forty-five. He inched it up to seventy and heard a click, followed somewhere in the house by a *whump*, then felt the satisfying rush of warm dusty air from the vents. The gas furnace was working still, so hopefully he wouldn't need the firewood out back. Unless the power went out, in which case the blower wouldn't work. And he didn't even want to think about that, especially after Mr. Saunders told him it could take days to be restored. Days with no internet, no TV, no computer...it would be enough to drive a modern man crazy.

But at least the bar was well-stocked. And there were neat rows of books on the shelves by the fireplace – many he had never read. If nothing else he could catch up on his reading while he enjoyed the solitude.

He took a deep breath. Yes. This would be a good couple of months. He could feel it.

II

Mirage

DARKNESS BEGAN TO FALL around four-thirty.

Lee heated a frozen dinner in the microwave and sat at the dining room table, watching the sun set in a glow of pink and red and eating a barely digestible glob of mushy spaghetti and meatballs. It certainly wasn't the best food he'd ever eaten, but the lack of tension and barely-sustained hostility from Jessie made for a more comfortable meal. He leaned back in his chair and stared out at the water. He'd tuned the radio to the classical station in Springfield, and strains of a Bach concerto wafted through the house. Though Jessie was a trained pianist, she had never appreciated Lee's near-obsessive fondness for music. She'd tolerated it over the years, but more often than not she was always asking him to turn it down, whether it was a light symphony or thundering rock. The past few months he'd taken to wearing headphones constantly, both to keep the peace and to tune her out.

Funny. He hadn't realized until today how much he had come to resent her, how trapped she made him feel. How inferior. If it weren't for Lizbeth and Corey he could end the marriage now. Let her keep the house in the city and he could stay here at the lake. It would be perfect. And probably best for both of them. But he couldn't let go of the kids. Not now, not ever. He was determined to be there for them, even if he and Jessie had to sleep in separate rooms for the next fifteen years.

And yet here he was, running off to find solitude and leaving them behind. But it wasn't permanent, and that made it different. Just two months. Eight weeks. And then he'd be back. And maybe his absence would be good for Jessie. Maybe she would see the void he left. Maybe she would understand how she had pushed him away, what a bitch she'd been. And maybe she would welcome him back with a newfound love, the kind she'd shone when they first began dating.

But maybe he didn't want that anymore. Maybe it was time for him to move on. To either find someone else or embrace a new life as a single man.

Either way, this two months was going to tell the tale. It was more than about writing, and both he and Jessie knew that. There was a lot riding on this, both personally and professionally, and for the first time he realized how much he was pressuring himself over this sabbatical. And that kind of pressure wasn't conducive to either writing or to figuring out what the hell he was doing with his life. He had to just go with whatever this time brought, good or bad, and not force it. He'd tried forcing things for over a year now, and that hadn't worked out at all. And wasn't the whole purpose of coming here to generate a different mindset, to jolt his brain into thinking in new directions?

Outside, night had fallen in earnest, and the patio doors reflected back a disheveled, unshaven red-haired man sitting at the dining room table with a half-eaten frozen dinner and an empty bottle of wine. He grimaced at himself. God, he looked homeless.

He cleaned the table and left the fork in the sink, then trudged upstairs to take a shower. The bedroom was dark and smelled of waxed pine and stale linens, and if he closed his eyes he could catch a slight scent of Jessie's perfume. Like a ghost.

A black shape loomed in the corner. He reached blindly for the lamp on the nightstand, switching it on but knocking it askance in the process. Light flooded the room and he was relieved to see the shape was only his own reflection in the cheval mirror. The mirror had been in the same location for years, but each time he entered the room it took him by surprise as if he'd never seen it before. He took a deep breath. All that talk by Mr. Saunders had set him on edge, and now he was seeing menace in every shadow, hearing intruders in every creak and groan of the floorboards. He had to get hold of himself. He was tired and stressed. A good, hot shower and everything would be better.

He stood under the water, feeling the tension dissipate from his neck and shoulders, running his soapy fingers across his chest and stomach and wishing they were Jessie's. Or anyone's, for that matter. It had been so long since he had felt the touch of someone else, and sometimes his body practically ached for intimacy. But tonight he was too tired anyway, even for himself, and all he wanted was to get dried off and settled comfortably with a book. Once out of the shower, he wiped the fog from the mirror and filled up the sink for a shave. But as he stared at himself, he decided he liked the dusting of copper-colored whiskers across his cheeks and chin; it defined his face and made him look a little rugged. Jessie had never cared for facial hair and since they'd been married he had always been cleanshaven. But now he might just grow a full beard. Fuck it. He drained the water from the sink and finished drying off.

He pulled on a faded pair of jeans and an old sweater and made his way back downstairs. The radio station had traded Bach for Beethoven – the sixth symphony. He could never hear this anymore without thinking of those flying horses and charging centaurs from Disney's *Fantasia*, and how Lizbeth would sit mesmerized in front of the television through the whole sequence. He ignored the sudden stab of hurt and poured himself a liberal dose of Jim Beam in the kitchen. The whiskey's warmth raced through his chest and abdomen, and he took another sip for good measure.

He blew dust off the volumes lined along the bookshelves, absently thinking he should really take tomorrow and give the house a good cleaning, and pulled out a collection of Poe's stories. It had been a while since he had visited old Edgar, and tonight seemed a perfect time to renew their kinship. It was a handsome book, leather-bound with gilded pages, illustrated throughout with vintage pen-and-ink drawings. It had been a present from Jessie back in their first year of marriage, back when they were actually putting some thought into their gift-giving and not just buying random crap for the sake of obligation.

He nestled into a corner of the sofa, drink in hand and reading glasses perched on his nose, and leafed through the pages until he found "The Tell-Tale Heart," one of his favorites. The claustrophobic feel and the paranoia of the narrator was near genius, and no matter how many times Lee read it he was always amazed at Poe's mastery. But tonight the words began to swim, whether from his fatigue or the bourbon or the hypnotizing strains of the Beethoven, he didn't know. The book's illustrations, bold and eerie and gory with their skeletal black-eyed figures and rich art-nouveau settings, unnerved him. He closed the book and set it on the coffee table, then leaned back against the sofa cushions, his glass resting on his belly. Another sip of bourbon and he closed his eyes, letting the symphony (the *Pastoral*, he remembered) float through his mind.

And then he was in the mythological world of the Disney cartoon, except instead of the happy Technicolor illustrations the land was infested with the gangly, rotting black-and-white creatures from the Poe book. He was naked. A light-haired maiden approached him, her robes whipping in an unfelt wind, her hollow eyes ringed with dark ink, her limbs snaking out like some putrid liquid. And only when she touched him with those bone-white hands did he dare gaze into her face. And saw Jessie. She opened her mouth and from the black depths poured forth a torrent of dark insects, their wings fluttering and clicking, and only when they took to the sky did he realize they were fireflies, their bodies pulsing red against the colorless sky. He looked back to Jessie, but her face held no expression. She reached a bony hand toward his face, caressed his cheek. Then plunged her fingers into his chest. Blood erupted, thick and dark. And Jessie smiled as she held up his heart. It was still beating where it sat in the palm of her hand. She leaned closer, as if to kiss him. But suddenly her mouth yawned open and he was lost in its black void.

He came awake with a start, aware that his body was wet with blood. But as he sat up he realized he'd only spilled the bourbon across his chest. His glasses were askew on his face, and he pulled them off and set them on top of the book. The radio station had signed off for the night and the symphony had been replaced with static. He snapped off the radio and set his empty glass in the kitchen sink, then turned out the lamp and headed upstairs to bed.

In the bedroom he pulled out of his soaked sweater and draped it over the side of the tub to dry, then stepped out of his jeans and crawled between the cold sheets. And just as he turned out the light he remembered he'd forgotten to brush his teeth. Well, fuck it. Missing one night wasn't going hurt him. And besides, the bourbon probably killed anything that was swimming around his mouth anyway.

He closed his eyes and drifted immediately into a deep and thankfully dreamless sleep.

● ● ●

He awoke suddenly, his heart thudding in his chest, and he immediately remembered the dream from earlier, of Jessie's horrifying smile as she held his still-beating heart in her hand.

The room was pitch-dark and cold. The digital clock on the nightstand read 3:27.

He lay staring at the ceiling, trying to will himself

back to sleep, but the images from the nightmare kept flashing across his vision. There were some deep-seated psychological issues there to be sure. Dr. Thayer would have a field day with that one.

He turned over onto his side, facing the window. It was a moonless night, and nothing, not even the weak glow of the walkway lights out back seemed to penetrate into the room. He'd never been afraid of the dark, not even as a kid, but something about the blackness of the room tonight bothered him, as if the night were a living thing that had seeped into his room, surrounded the bed and was reaching out for him. A chill racked his body and he snuggled deeper into the covers. He'd checked the thermostat on his way up and set it to seventy. So why was it so damned cold?

Must be nerves. He was freaking himself out. Between Mr. Saunders' stories, the drawings in the Poe book, and the bourbon-fueled nightmare, he was scaring himself silly. Here he was, thirty-nine years old and jumping at shadows. He really had to get a grip on himself. How the hell was he going to survive two months here alone when he was already going psycho the first night?

He took a deep breath and closed his eyes. He lay as still as he could, concentrating on the cadence of his heartbeat, the sound of air flowing in and out of his lungs, the heaviness of his limbs. The softness of the blankets piled around him. The comforting scent of his pillow.

And just as he started to drift off, the scratching brought him fully awake.

He flopped over on his back, staring into the nothingness and straining to hear it again.

It came with more insistence and a steady, grinding rhythm.

He sat up and cocked his ear. It seemed to be coming from directly over his head, above the ceiling. There was nothing up there but unfinished attic. He refused to let himself think of squatters or vandals, no matter what nonsense Mr. Saunders had filled his head with. And besides, a human would be making more noise than that. This was gnawing. A mouse. Or a rat. Or even a squirrel. Some kind of rodent.

He sat looking up for a moment. The sound was incessant. Relentless. He hated the idea of crawling up through the attic entrance in the hall closet in the middle of the night to confront whatever animal was making that noise, but if he was going to get any sleep tonight there might not be a choice.

He blew out a breath and swung his legs out of the bed into the cold, then switched on the bedside lamp.

The scratching stopped.

He sat still as stone, waiting for the noise to resume but it didn't. Nor did he hear any rustling or pattering of tiny rodent feet. There was nothing. No sound at all.

After a minute or two he turned out the lamp and hunkered down beneath the blankets again, his brain on a hair-trigger to pop awake at the slightest noise.

But everything stayed quiet, and eventually sleep overtook him.

* * *

He awoke to the gray light of an overcast sky that barely filtered through the windows. He lay staring at the wooden beams crossing the ceiling, remembering the gnawing during the night. He supposed he would have to look up there for signs of rodents. And that would most likely call for a trip into town to the hardware store for traps or poison. Nasty for sure, but he couldn't very well let mice take over his house.

He crawled from the bed, shivering and stretching, and made his way to the bathroom. His bladder was full to bursting. As he relieved himself, he glanced at the gray sweater draped over the side of the tub. The bourbon had left a yellowish stain in the center of it, and he cursed himself for not rinsing it out.

He rinsed his hands in the sink, then splashed the cold water across his face, surprised at first at the feel of the scruff beneath his fingers. Oh, yeah. He was going to let his beard grow out. Jessie be damned. He looked at himself in the mirror and grinned, then stared in horror at what he saw.

In the center of his chest, beneath the patch of auburn hair, was a puckered wound, crusted with dried blood. He grazed it with his fingertips. It was tender and sore. He grabbed a washcloth from the shelf and moistened it, then dabbed at the spot until the area was clean. He stared at it. It was round, about the size of the pad of his thumb, and was puffy and pink like an old scar. But he'd never had an injury there. And there was no broken skin, nothing to warrant the dried blood.

It was the same spot where Jessie had ripped out his heart in the dream.

That was impossible. It must be some psychological reaction. Some physical manifestation of the terror he'd felt in the dream. Hives or something. He took one more glance at the wound and decided he wouldn't worry about it. If it got worse he'd go to the doctor.

The bedroom was freezing. He hurriedly slipped into

his jeans and a sweatshirt, then padded downstairs to make coffee. He needed warmth and nourishment.

The thermostat was still set at seventy; he slid it up a notch to seventy-two and paused with his finger on the button until he heard the furnace kick on. Warm air flowed from the vents as he passed into the kitchen, but it didn't seem to penetrate his skin. He shivered as he prepared the coffee maker and stood huddled over the pot as it brewed. And when it had finished, he poured himself a cup and stood in front of the patio doors, staring at the churning gray lake and the equally gray skies above it. A mist hid the shore on the other side, giving the illusion that the cabin was completely isolated. An island surrounded by water and fog.

The silence was deafening.

He switched on the radio. The station was playing a modern classical piece he couldn't remember the name of. It was dark and clashing and brash, and it suddenly occurred to him that it was by Penderecki, and he knew it from being included in Kubrick's movie *The Shining*. Strings slid down the scale like melting wax, capped off with climbing woodwinds. He moved the dial and found a country station, but after a couple of minutes of yee-haw and country girls in cut-off jeans, he snapped the music off. Even the silence was better than that.

When he'd finished his coffee, he grabbed a flashlight and wound his way back upstairs to the hallway closet. He pulled the string attached to the hanging bulb and the space flooded with light. The entrance to the attic was here, a simple square hole blocked by a crude cover constructed of two-by-fours and stained ceiling tiles. He climbed up on a small stool from one of the other bedrooms and slid the panel to one side. Stale, cool air wafted down, along with dust and the smell of old wood. He poked his head up into the darkness and shined the light into the opening.

Nothing. The area was barely big enough for a man to crawl in. The beams supporting the roof were unmarked and the dim light filtering in through the eave vents showed them to be solid. The aluminum ductwork snaked through the space, reflecting back the flashlight like something from a science fiction movie. Below that, just atop the ceilings of the bedrooms, the baffles of pink insulation lay undisturbed between the rafters. He focused the beam on the area where the gnawing had come from last night, just above his bed. But there was nothing out of the ordinary. No teeth marks on the wood, no signs of any kind of rodent nest, not even a stray turd.

Could an animal have been on the roof trying to gain entrance to the attic?

He closed up the opening and headed downstairs. He wanted to take a closer look at the outside of the house.

He slipped on his boots and stepped out onto the front stoop. In spite of the chill in the house, the air outside seemed almost balmy, especially for January. The mist from the lake had enveloped the front of the house as well. The skeletal limbs of the trees at the edge of the woods seemed to be clawing their way through the fog, as if trying to escape whatever was lurking in it. Somewhere a crow cawed and was answered by another, a desperate, lonely sound. He licked his lips and tasted the bitter residue of the coffee, then pulled the collar of his sweatshirt closer around his neck and stepped off to the side of the house.

He walked the perimeter around the house, scanning

the metal roof and the aluminum soffits and fascia; all appeared solid. There were no visible signs of rot or animal disturbance. Nothing to indicate anything had tried to gnaw its way in.

There were twin-dimpled tracks in the soft earth at the edge of the driveway where a deer had crossed through the yard at some point in the night. He followed them to where they disappeared into the brush at the edge of the forest. The fog in the woods seemed thicker now, and he could barely see beyond a few feet in front of him. The trunks of the trees were vague, dark shapes hulking in the gray. He realized he was still holding the flashlight, and he resisted the urge to turn it on.

A twig snapped, and he followed the sound with a jerk of his head. Something was moving through the woods. Something big and heavy, and he sighed with relief when he realized it was probably just the deer. God, he was back to jumping at shadows again. He really needed to get a grip on himself.

"Hey there."

He spun around, reflexively bringing up the flashlight as a weapon.

It was an older burly man, dressed in denim bib overalls and a Carhartt jacket. White hair splayed out from beneath a tattered John Deere cap. "Sorry, didn't mean to startle you." He stuck out a large rough hand and Lee shook it, surprised at how it swallowed up his own. "Harvey Compton. I live just up the road."

"Lee Houston." He was ashamed at how the jolt of Harvey's voice had sent his heart into panic mode.

"You're the writer, ain't ya?"

Lee nodded. "Guilty as charged."

"Seen you folks around a few times, mostly in the summer."

"Yeah, we don't get out here too much during the winter," Lee said.

"Not many people do."

"I think I've seen you once or twice."

"Probably out walking. I do a lot of that."

"I came out to stay for a few weeks and get some writing done," Lee said.

Harvey raised an eyebrow. "By yourself?"

"Yeah." Lee noticed the tone of disapproval, the same one he'd detected with Mr. Saunders, and he was in no mood for a lecture. "I'll be all right. I promise."

Harvey threw his hands up. "Not saying a word. I just know how lonely it can get out here when you get snowed in."

Lee chuckled, then nodded toward the house. "I just made a pot of coffee. Want to join me?"

"Sure." Harvey followed Lee back toward the front stoop. "Saw you looking around your roof. Everything all right?"

"Far as I can tell." Lee held the door open and Harvey slipped inside. "Thought I might have a critter up in the attic."

"Critter?" Harvey shrugged out of his coat and Lee hung it on a hook by the front door. "Like a coon or something?"

"Don't know." Lee led the way toward the kitchen and pulled down a clean cup, filled it with coffee and slid it over the counter to Harvey. "Heard something up there last night. Sounded like it was gnawing on something. Had a look this morning, but everything checked out okay." He offered cream and sugar, but

Harvey declined it. "And I didn't see anything outside that looked like anything might have tried to get in."

Harvey took a seat on a barstool and leaned over his cup. "Well, who knows. Squirrels, mice, rats... they can get in through the tiniest spaces. Had a family of owls in my attic one time."

"Really?" Lee said. "Owls?"

Harvey nodded, chuckling. "Had to get the Wildlife Department out here to get them out."

"Wow."

"And do you know the government bastards had the gall to send me a bill for two hundred and fifty dollars for it?"

"You're kidding."

Harvey shook his head and sipped his coffee. "Nope. A fee for 'relocation of wildlife' or somesuch bullshit."

"Did you pay it?"

Harvey looked at him. "Wasn't going to. But then I figured they'd find some way to get it out of me anyhow."

Lee nodded. "Most likely."

Harvey leaned back on the stool. "So...all by your lonesome here, huh?"

"Yep." Lee sloshed out the cold coffee from earlier into the sink and refilled his cup. "Got a new project I need to get on."

"Wife didn't want to come?"

Lee looked at him, then back at his cup. "No."

"Ah," Harvey said. He looked away. "Sorry. Didn't mean to pry."

"It's all right," Lee said. "I think we both needed some time away from each other."

"I get that."

Lee blew on his coffee, then took a sip. He eyed the wedding band on the older man's hand. "So what about you? How long you and your wife lived out here?"

Harvey blew out a breath. "I live alone. My wife passed away six years ago."

"Oh. Sorry."

Harvey shook his head. "No need." He ran a thumb around the rim of his cup. "We bought our place out here back in the 'eighties, when our kids were still teenagers and Gail and I still had the energy to try to keep up with 'em. I retired about ten years ago, and we sold our house in Cedar Hill and decided to stay out here permanent."

"So you live alone?"

"Yep." Harvey took a sip from his cup. "That's why I said I know how lonely it can get out here in the winter. Damn near drive a man crazy when a big snow comes."

Lee laughed. "That's just what Mr. Saunders said up at the general store."

Harvey looked at him with his penetrating gray eyes, unsmiling. "It's the truth."

"Well, I appreciate the concern, but I'm looking forward to the solitude. I'm a writer, remember? I need all the peace and quiet I can get."

Harvey nodded and chuckled. "All right. But if you need anything I'm just a phone call away." He dug a small notepad and a pen from the pocket of his overalls and scrawled his number, then slid the paper over to Lee.

Lee looked at the note and nodded. He had no idea how an overweight seventy-something man could help him in a real emergency, but he wasn't going to question it.

Harvey looked toward the patio doors, to the white wall of fog outside. It had grown thicker and now completely obscured the lake. "Not much of a view today, huh?"

Lee grunted. "Yeah, I was surprised to see that this morning. Yesterday was beautiful, even if it was colder."

"Supposed to rain tomorrow," Harvey said.

"That so? I haven't looked at a forecast."

"Yep. Quite a soaker, from what I hear." He drained his cup and set it down. "Guess I'd better get moving along." He slid off the stool and headed toward the front door.

"Don't rush off," Lee said, following him.

"Well, I'm sure you've got work to do. I know I do." He opened the door and paused on the threshold, slipping on his jacket and looking back at Lee. "I guess Saunders told you about some of the break-ins we get out here during the off-season."

"Yeah, he mentioned that." Lee thought about the desecration of the Millers' house and pushed it from his mind. "I'm not worried."

"Never had anybody try to get in my house, but I've seen evidence of 'em prowling around. Beer cans, cigarette butts, that kinda stuff."

"I'll be careful. It's probably just kids from town."

"Maybe," Harvey said. "But I wouldn't bet my life on it. You keep an eye out."

"I will."

Harvey stared off into the fog. "You know, that lake trail is a public right-of-way. Never agreed with that. Some of us tried to fight it back in the 'nineties but we never got anywhere. I don't mind people using it who live out here, but I never thought just any yahoo should be able to traipse up and down it, looking into people's houses and leaving their trash everywhere. And they do. Especially in the summer. Sometimes we get a couple of townies out here tearing it up with four-wheelers, but thank God that's rare. At least on this end of the lake." He looked back at Lee and grunted. "Well, I've talked your ear off long enough. I'll see you around."

"Come back any time," Lee told him. "I mean that."

Harvey was already shuffling down the drive. He waved a hand and disappeared into the mist.

Lee shivered as a sudden chill racked his body. It wasn't really cold out today. Not at all. So why was he so fucking cold? He took one last look at the fog and shut the door. The thermostat still said seventy-two, but damn if it didn't feel warmer outside than in the house.

In the dining area, he pulled out his laptop and set it on the table, angling it so he could look out across the lake and see the screen at the same time. Except of course now he could see nothing but white past the deck railing. The silence was heavy, heavy as the fog outside, and if it hadn't been for Harvey's visit, he would have felt like the last man on earth. He fired up the laptop and watched it boot to Windows, clasping his fingers around the warmth of his coffee cup; his fingers were like ice.

He connected to the wi-fi and opened his email, watching the messages appear one by one, and he felt a sting of panic when he saw one from Bill Cosgrove. He clicked on it.

From: Bill Cosgrove <bill@cosgroveliterary.com>
To: Lee Houston <houston3@rronline.com>
Sent: Friday, January 5 6:32 PM
Subject: Checking In

Hey Lee, just checking on you. Wanted to see where you are on the new project. Anything you can tell me yet? Tom Feeney and the other folks at Circle are getting antsy for some news. I think I've put them off about as long as I can. I was hoping you and I could have a phone conference next week sometime. I'll be available Tuesday or Wednesday from 9 until 3 eastern, or if neither of those days works for you, we can try for another time. One evening if need be.

Look, I don't have to tell you that you're in a tight spot. We've been stalling for almost a year and a half now and I'll be honest with you. You're in danger of being dropped by Circle. And if that happens there's probably nothing I or any other agent can do to get you back in good graces with New York. The publishing environment has changed quite a bit since we started working together. It's no longer about your reputation as a writer or your reviews or your past accomplishments; it all boils down to whether you can deliver the goods and make money for the next quarter. Being dropped by Circle doesn't mean we could just go to another house and pick up where we left off. You'd have to look at using a pseudonym or consider self-publishing. And the advance Circle gave you on the new three-book contract would have to be repaid. And frankly, if it comes to that, I would have to drop you as a client for any future projects.

You're a good writer, Lee. Our association has been very beneficial to both of us. I don't want to see any of this happen. But it's crunch time now, and we need a game plan. I hope I don't come off as harsh, but you need a good dose of reality.

Let me know if either of those days will work.

Bill

Lee sat looking at the screen, feeling numb.
You need a good dose of reality.
He supposed that was true. And Bill had always been honest with him. He hastily composed a reply, setting ten o-clock Tuesday morning as a meeting time. Best to get it over with as soon as possible. He hit the "send" button before he could change his mind.

He closed out the email and opened Word and stared at the blank screen, at the blinking cursor. Feeling the sluggishness in his brain, as if all the gears had seized and left his thoughts paralyzed.

Breakfast. He needed something to eat. Maybe that would help.

In the kitchen he pulled the box of Pop Tarts from the cabinet and ripped into them, not bothering to heat them. He took a bite and grimaced. Frosted cherry. What had he been thinking?

His cell phone vibrated on the table and he moved to grab it. His heart skipped a beat when he saw Jessie's name on the screen. "Hey."

"Hey," she said. "Get settled in?"

He slumped into the chair in front of the laptop and gazed out into the gray nothingness beyond the patio doors. "Yeah. Just having some breakfast."

"Breakfast? Lee, it's after one."

Shit. He looked at the clock in the corner of his monitor. 1:18. "Wow. I hadn't even looked at the time. I guess I slept later than I thought. It's so foggy here today, I can barely tell the sun's out."

"Really? The sun's bright here. Hard to believe it's supposed to rain tomorrow."

"Guess it's something weird with the lake." He listened to the uncomfortable silence for a moment. "It was lonely here last night."

Jessie sighed. "Well, it was your decision to go down there."

"I know. It's just so. . . damned quiet."

"Isn't that what you wanted?"

He shivered. "And I can't get warm. Didn't we have the system checked out last summer?"

"Yeah, I think so."

"I don't think it's working right. The thermostat says it's seventy-two in here but I'm freezing. What's the name of that guy that serviced it last year?"

"I don't know. Chuck something-or-other. I'll have to look for it. I wrote it down."

"Do that. And let me know when you find it."

"Okay." There was a pause, and he could hear voices in the background. "Here," Jessie said, "Corey wants to talk to you."

There was a shuffle and Corey's voice came over the phone. "Hey, Dad."

"Hey, sport. Seen any more fireflies?"

"Nope."

"Me neither."

"When are you coming home?"

Lee grunted. "I've only been gone one night."

"Seems like forever."

"I know." Lee minimized the window on his computer and looked at the background picture on his desktop. The four of them in happier days, last spring on the cruise to Cozumel, captured by one of the ship's photographers beside the pool in the Caribbean sun. All in their bathing suits, all smiling heartily at the camera. Even Jessie. That was when he thought the two of them still might have a chance. When even though things weren't going great it appeared they might still be able to salvage what was left. They'd managed to be alone twice on that trip, both times while the kids were away at activities somewhere else on the ship. Their lovemaking had felt furious and desperate, as if they were trying to grasp the relationship that was slipping through their fingers. But in the end they had both let go, and they hadn't been intimate since.

"Macbeth keeps walking around the house meowing," Corey said. "I think he's looking for you."

Lee winced, thinking of the slain cat at the Millers'. "Well, you tell him I'll be back in a few weeks. And tell him I could use a good cat like him. I think I may have a mouse in my house."

Corey giggled. "Really?"

"Yeah. I'm gonna try to do something about that today."

"Oh, don't hurt him."

"Well, maybe I can catch him and put him outside."

"Okay." There was a pause, and then Corey said, "Can I come stay with you?"

Lee took a deep breath. "You have school. And I've got to get some work done."

"Okay."

Lee looked at Corey's face in the photo. "Maybe you could come out next weekend."

"Really?"

"Yeah. We can spend the day together and you could stay the night."

"That would be great."

"Okay. I'll talk to your mother about it before then."

There was a muffled mumbling, and then Corey said, "Lizbeth wants to talk to you."

"Sure. We'll talk before next weekend, okay, sport?"

"'Bye, Dad."

Then Lizbeth took the phone. "Hey."

Lee felt a wave of hurt and anger. "Hey there."

"Sorry I didn't say goodbye yesterday."

"It's all right," Lee told her, though he didn't mean it.

"Are you getting some writing done?"

Lee stared at the laptop screen. "Yes, I am," he told her, the lie sailing from his lips without a thought.

"That's good," she said. "I've been thinking about my birthday. I'd like to have a party."

Jesus, he'd forgotten all about Lizbeth's birthday at the end of the month. "Well, take it up with your mom."

"I did. She said to ask you if you cared. It'll probably be a sleepover. Just two or three of my friends."

"Fine with me." At least he wouldn't have to be there to police it all night.

"Will you come home for the party?"

"Sure," he said. "I wouldn't miss it." He dragged his cursor around the screen of the laptop, circling Lizbeth's face. "What do you think you want for your birthday?"

"A new laptop," she said. "My old one's getting funky. And the 'E' key doesn't work half the time."

"Well, that one's three years old now. It's probably time to get rid of it. Start looking around for what you want and show it to your mom."

"I already know what I want. An iBook. It's what Taylor Swift used to write all her first songs on."

Lee chuckled. Lizbeth was the only other person in the household who came remotely close to Lee's love of music. "Okay, we'll see. Talk it over with your mother." He glanced outside at the fog. "Does she want to talk to me some more?"

Lizbeth cupped her hand over the phone and said something unintelligible, then came back. "No. She said she's done."

Something stabbed at him, and he wondered if Jessie meant done with the conversation or if her words had a deeper meaning. "Okay," he said. "I'll talk to you guys later."

"'Bye, Dad."

Lee disconnected the call and set the phone on the table. So she didn't want to talk to him. Then why did she call? For the kids? Was she checking up on him, or what? Well, fuck her. It was like she enjoyed playing with him, teasing him. Just the way cats did with mice before pouncing for the kill.

Mice. He needed to do something about whatever was gnawing last night. Even though he hadn't seen anything in the attic, there had to be some kind of animal making that noise. He'd go to the hardware store this afternoon and find some traps. Maybe poison.

He reached for his Pop Tart to take another bite and felt a pain in his chest so sharp and sudden that he dropped the pastry to the floor. His hand instinctively grasped at his shirt collar and came away slick with blood. He stared at the red smear across his fingertips with horror, then realized the whole front of his shirt was soaked.

He stumbled from the table, knocking over the chair with a clatter and tore the sweatshirt off over his head. The puckered wound in the center of his chest was oozing blood, and had been for some time from the looks of it.

He made his way up to the bathroom, climbing the stairs two at a time, and stared at himself in the mirror. The gash wasn't any larger, but something had made it start bleeding again. He grabbed the washcloth draped over the side of the tub and blotted up the blood, then rinsed it out and pressed the wet cloth against his chest. After several minutes the bleeding stopped.

He felt around it gingerly with his fingertips, afraid to press too hard and start it oozing blood again. But as closely as he looked, he was damned if he could find anywhere the skin was broken. The wound was still puckered and pink, but the flesh appeared whole.

So where was the fucking blood coming from?

He rooted around the bathroom drawers until he found a pack of gauze and medical tape – Jessie's first aid kit for the kids' summertime scraped knees and cuts. The square sheets covered the injury perfectly, and he taped the edges down, wondering how he would pull the bandage off later without ripping the hair off his chest. He thought again of going to the doctor, but he wasn't sure what could be done for a wound that spontaneously seeped blood without any apparent trauma.

He rinsed the sweatshirt in the sink as best as he could, although it looked as if the shirt was a goner. Maybe once it was laundered it wouldn't be too bad. He draped it over the side of the tub with the sweater. He hadn't been here two days yet and he'd already ruined half his wardrobe.

He slipped on a t-shirt, then pulled on another sweater. He was still freezing, and if he couldn't get warm soon he would have to put on his coat.

Downstairs, the fog had dissipated somewhat, and at least now he could see the water lapping the edge of the shore. He cleaned up the remnants of the dropped Pop Tart and drained what was left of his coffee. Maybe he should go on to the hardware store while he was thinking about it.

He grabbed his keys and his jacket and headed out to the Escalade. The mist out front was all but gone, and he wondered whether the cold water of the lake against the mass of warm air that had moved in would have caused it. Which would make sense that it was retreating as the sun heated up the water. As he drove up toward the main highway, the fog lifted and he saw a bright cloudless sky through the towering green pines. There were several cars at the general store as he made the turn toward town, and he thought about stopping by to see Mr. Saunders, but he didn't feel like getting another lecture today.

In Harper's Lake, the usual assortment of men had congregated outside Kesterson's Hardware, and they stared as he climbed out of the Escalade and made his way toward the front door. "How you fellas doing?" he said.

One of them, a large young buck with a full bushy dark beard nodded. "Out enjoying this weather before it turns cold again."

"Foggy on the other side of the lake," Lee said.

"Yep," the big guy said. "Gonna rain tomorrow. Then it's gonna snow."

"Really?" Lee said. "Snow?"

"That's what they say. A 'significant winter storm' I believe is what the weatherman called it."

"I heard we'd get anywhere from ten to fifteen inches," an older man said from where he leaned back against the building.

"Shit, if we get that much I'm stayin' in 'til spring," another said.

Lee chuckled and entered the store. A motion-activated beep signaled his presence and a squat burly man with a flannel shirt and a thick dark goatee appeared from behind the shelves. "Help ya?" He was holding a chrome pipe in a thick hand and looked to be anywhere from thirty to sixty.

"Looking for some poison." And when the other man raised an eyebrow, Lee added quickly, "Mouse poison."

"Ah." He pointed with the pipe. "Aisle three."

Lee made his way through the displays of roof shingles and paint chips to the pest control aisle and scanned the shelves until he found what he needed. The box promised the rodents would ingest the poison then leave the premises searching for water. Good. He didn't want dead animals stinking up the place. He grabbed the yellow box and headed back to the front counter where the other man was waiting for him. "Got it."

The goateed man took the box and smiled. "You're Lee Houston, aren't you?"

Lee nodded. "That's me."

The other man extended his hand and Lee shook it. "Kevin Kesterson. Proud owner of this fine establishment." He rung up the sale. "My kids love your books." He looked at Lee and gave a shy smile. "Well, actually, me and the wife do, too."

Lee chuckled. Over the years he'd become accustomed to adults admitting to enjoying Max Plexico, often with hushed voices and furtive glances, as if they were proclaiming a penchant for pornography. They seemed almost ashamed of finding pleasure in a children's story.

Kevin slid the box into a bag and placed it on the counter. "We've read all the books, seen all the movies... The kids are usually here at the store on the weekends. They'll be sorry they missed you."

Lee grabbed the bag. "Well, tell them I said hello." He turned to the front door, but stopped himself. "Say, you know where my house is, right?"

"Yep. Other side of the lake. Glen Cove Road."

Lee leaned against the counter. "What happened out there at the Millers' house last year? Mr. Saunders at the general store told me there was some trouble. Said someone broke in there and killed a cat, messed up the place."

Kevin nodded. "Yeah, it was bad business. Never did find out who did it. The local religious crazies'll tell you it was some kind of cult. The stories going around town were everything from animal sacrifice to Satanic worship."

"Mr. Saunders said there was a pentagram on the floor."

Kevin chuckled. "He probably also told you it was drawn in human blood, didn't he?"

Lee smiled. "Yeah, he did."

Kevin shook his head. "I don't know where he heard that, but it's not true."

"He said the sheriff – "

"I know the sheriff," Kevin said, holding up a hand. "Personally. We went to high school together. There was no pentagram. No human blood."

Lee nodded, starting to feel foolish that he'd let Mr. Saunders' stories get to him. "No dead cat either, I suppose."

"Oh, they did kill a cat," Kevin said. "Wrote some cuss words on the wall with its blood. Trashed the house. General vandalism."

Lee felt himself relax. "So no Satanic rituals?"

Kevin laughed. "Look, Harper's Lake has had its share of crazy things happen over the years. Murders, suicides, robberies. But no cult activity that I've ever been aware of, and I've lived here all my life. It's a pretty quiet little place, even in the summer when it gets crowded."

"Well, that makes me feel a little better."

"I've known Mr. Saunders since I was a kid," Kevin said, scratching his chin through his beard. "He's a good man, but he likes to gossip. He likes to *sensationalize*, you know what I mean? Don't let him spook you."

Lee nodded. "Thanks."

Outside, a balmy breeze was blowing in from the lake, and across the water he could see the fog shrouding the far shore like a gray blanket. The other men followed his gaze. "Does fog usually behave like that?" he asked them.

"It happens," the young buck said, keeping his eyes on the mist. "Usually burns off by this time of day, though."

"My granny always said when a low fog hovers over the water until evening, there's gonna be a death."

Lee looked to see who had spoken. It was the older man leaning against the wall of the building. His face was dusted with gray scruff, and his thinning white hair splayed across his head. He shifted his gaze to Lee, and Lee saw that one of the man's eyes was gone. In its place was a pink empty socket that glistened in the afternoon sun. Lee felt a sting of revulsion, and ducked past the group, eager for the cocoon of the Escalade. The men watched as he started the vehicle and backed out of the lot, and in his rearview mirror he saw them go back to their conversation.

Back at the cabin, he climbed into the attic and opened the package of poison, placing one of the tan waxy bars close to the trap door. Peanut butter flavor.

He'd always heard mice liked peanut butter. "Take that, you little bastards," he said. He only hoped that when the rodents searched for water they would head out toward the lake.

In the bathroom, he scrubbed his hands beneath scalding water. The soiled clothing draped over the side of the tub caught his eye, and when he had dried his hands he lifted his sweater and t-shirt to look at the wound on his chest. The bandage was pristine and nothing had soaked through. He resisted the urge to yank off the dressing and look at the wound again, both knowing he could aggravate it and start it bleeding again and fearful of what he might see.

Downstairs, the cursor still blinked on the blank page on the laptop. He sat for a moment and stared at it, feeling a weight settle on his shoulders. Words seemed to evade him. Ideas, worn and clichéd, floated through his head, but nothing he could grasp and twist into something original. He placed his fingers on the keyboard and typed

The night was

He stared at it. The night was what? And suddenly he remembered Billy Crystal struggling with writing the same sentence in *Throw Momma from the Train* and he laughed. God, his mind was so clouded he was pulling lines from old movies.

He pushed away from the table and found himself staring out the patio doors. The fog still hovered just past the shore line, obscuring everything but just a few feet of the water. He grabbed his jacket and stepped out onto the deck, amazed again at how much warmer the outside felt compared to the house. A large gathering of grackles in the side yard took flight at his sudden appearance, the combined roar of their wings almost like distant cannon fire.

He trudged down the steps, across the brown grass, and headed down the slope toward the lake trail at the water's edge. It was a well-worn path, carpeted with yellowed pine needles and crunchy oak leaves, stretching both directions into the oblivion of the fog. The water lapped at the wooden dock, the only sound that reached his ears. He stepped out onto the planking and walked the length of the dock to end. They'd always said they would get a boat. Nothing fancy, just a pontoon for cruising the lake or fishing. But of course they never had. Jessie thought it a foolish expense and argued that they would never use it. So he'd relented, and the dock stayed empty.

Now, as he stood there enveloped in the mist, he realized how much he had allowed her to dictate their lives over the years, how many times he had yielded to her and let her have her way. How many times he had been miserable rather than confront her about her selfishness. But maybe that was all behind him now. This solo trip to the lake was the first spontaneous thing he had done since he was a kid. And it felt good. It felt liberating.

He reached the edge of the dock and looked back the way he had come. From here he couldn't see the house. Could barely see the shore in fact. He was in a white void, surrounded by nothingness.

My granny always said when a low fog hovers over the water until evening, there's gonna be a death.

He shivered, and immediately felt like a fool. That old one-eyed coot had just been trying to scare him. Probably got his rocks off spooking city people.

He headed back toward the trail, aware of how hollow and dull his steps sounded on the wood of the dock, and turned toward the east, only realizing after he started walking that he was going toward the Millers' place. He knew they would be gone; they were summer people like himself. And he didn't know what he expected to see. But the stories had his imagination going, and he felt a pull toward the house that he couldn't explain.

The trail wound up onto a small bluff overlooking the water. The woods stretched out on the other side of the trail, a thick stand of barren oaks and scraggly pines. The fog, thick as cotton, dulled the sound of the lapping water and the scurry of tiny animals through the trees. The ground was worn smooth here, as if this were a place hikers regularly stopped to take in the view.

A discarded cigarette butt lay in the dirt. It seemed fairly old. Lee nudged it with his toe and the filter tore into white shreds. He thought of faceless strangers wandering up and down the trail in the night and felt and stab of panic. He'd dealt with a stalker once, and he had no desire to go through that hell again. That had been an unstable young man, Cameron Fields, who had somehow found Lee's personal email address and cell phone number and sent him threatening messages and texts. The police had been unable to do anything, and Lee and Jessie had been forced to endure the constant barrage of abuse up until Fields, fully decked out in Max Plexico adventure gear, had followed them to a hotel in Memphis and tried to ram his way into their room. Hopefully the teenager – and by now he must be in his early-twenties, Lee thought – was safely ensconced in a hospital somewhere getting the help he desperately needed. He'd often wondered if Cameron Fields would ever show up again out of the blue after he was released. And if he did, Lee had no idea whether he could handle that again.

He left the lookout and made his way on up the trail, suddenly aware of how vulnerable he was here alone and unprotected. There could be anyone in these woods. Someone could be watching him at this moment, and he'd never see them hidden in the fog. After all, Harvey had appeared behind him earlier, and Lee had never heard him coming. The thought made him shiver. He stopped and peered into the gloom of the forest. Now instead of a squirrel scampering through the dead leaves he imagined he was hearing a person – perhaps Cameron Fields – lying in wait for him around the next bend, crouching in the brush, his feet rustling the undergrowth.

Good lord, he had to get hold of himself. It was starting to get dark now – dusk came early this time of year – and he didn't want to be caught out after sundown. It was already difficult enough to navigate through the mist, and he damn sure didn't want to be bumbling around out here in the pitch dark without a flashlight.

After a good few hundred yards' hike another boat dock appeared out of the fog. Like his own, this one was empty, but Lee knew the Millers owned a pontoon and always hauled it back home for the winter. He'd seen them cruising across the lake many times. David Miller, always shirtless and tanned; Linda usually wearing a bikini and looking quite fine; and Thomas swallowed by an enormous orange life vest, his head covered with a baseball cap. All three looking perfect and happy. They always waved. Always. And Lee wondered if the picture of contentment they projected was as false and forced as the one he imagined people saw in his own house. Did people see Jessie and him as a perfect couple? Wealthy and happy and loving? He'd heard people say they were a good match, and he wondered what those same people would say if they knew what really went on inside the walls of their home.

He blew out a breath. There was no reason to think about that now. He wasn't here to brood over his failing marriage. This was a time to be creative and let his mind wander unbridled. Fuck Jessie, and fuck his marriage. He would have plenty of time to deal with that once this sabbatical was over. And maybe by then he would be able to let go of his resentment and anger.

Sandstone steps led from the lake trail up the slope toward the house, which was only a vague shadow in the fog. He trudged up them, staring at the dark windows as they emerged, imagining someone peering out and watching him approach. There was no movement within the house that he could see, yet something about all that glass, stretching from the deck to the apex of the A-frame, unnerved him. Anyone could be in there watching from the shadows and he'd never see them.

The deck was littered with a scattering of dead oak leaves and cones from the towering pines around the property. Furniture sat wrapped in black tarps wound with nylon cording, and a grill was pushed against the redwood siding of the house. The deck was older than his own, and here and there gray boards buckled and squeaked as he walked over them. It was definitely due for some maintenance, maybe even replacing.

Beside the sliding door sat a small bike, and he wondered why they hadn't stored it somewhere out of the weather. He thought of Corey, who had just learned to ride without his training wheels last summer, and he felt a pang of longing. He hoped he would be able to bring Corey down here next weekend as he had promised. And for a split second he wondered if Jessie would try to talk him out of it. It seemed like something she would do – completely illogical and conceived only for the sole purpose of trying to control him and everything else.

He had no idea where this sudden hatred for her had come from, or when it had clouded over the love he once felt for her. He'd thought for a long time it had something to do with his sudden success with Max Plexico, but now as he pondered it, he saw that it had begun way before that. Maybe even before they were married.

Perhaps it was when he tried to substitute her for Kat, when he saw Kat was gone for good and he'd felt panicked that he would never find anyone else as perfect. When he thought he could mold life with Jessie into the ideal existence he'd imagined with Kat. When he realized that wasn't going to happen and he'd become disillusioned with the way things were turning out. When he realized he'd gone too far to simply abandon the relationship.

He stepped up to the sliding glass door and peered into the darkness beyond. In the dim light he could see a large sectional arranged around a stone fireplace and the vague suggestion of a kitchen behind that. An open balcony above appeared to house a sleeping loft. Lee rattled the sliding door and felt the satisfying hold of the latch. Everything seemed secure. He took one last peek inside, trying not to imagine the paneled walls smeared with cat's blood, and headed back down the steps toward the trail.

Darkness was falling quickly now, and with the dense fog the light seemed to merely fade; there was no sunset, no magnificent colors reflected off the lake. Just a steady gloom that gathered about him like a shroud. He would be lucky to make it back to the cabin before he could no longer see his way.

He passed the Millers' dock and rounded the bend where he had imagined Cameron Fields hiding, then plodded along the path toward home. As the light died, the growth on either side of the trail seemed to close in. Twice he felt his sweater snag on low-hanging branches, and he stifled a startled cry as he thought of Cameron's slender fingers grabbing hold of him. He realized he was walking at such a brisk pace he was practically jogging. But the unease in the back of his mind had ballooned into full-blown terror, and though the rational part of his brain that remained told him there was nothing to fear, it was drowned out by the thud of his panicked heart in his ears.

So when he topped the hill and spotted the dark mass huddled on the lookout where he'd stopped earlier, he practically leaped off the trail in fright.

Something lay across the trail, blocking the way. He froze mid-step, staring at the shape, watching for it to move, waiting for it to make a sound.

It did neither.

He inched toward it, ready to head into the woods should it make the slightest motion. But it did nothing.

And as he crept upon it, he realized why.

It was a deer. Dead. A buck with a large rack. Lee counted twelve points. Its torso was ripped open, spilling entangled intestines and a dark pool of blood across the path and exuding the suffocating metallic stench of blood. The buck's tongue lolled from its mouth and its lifeless eyes were glassy and black. Whatever had taken it down had done so in the last half hour, just in the time he had passed this way, looked around the Millers', and returned. And whatever had done it had been big. Maybe a bobcat. Lee must have frightened it off before it could feed.

He looked about, straining his ears for the sound of anything moving through the woods. If the cat thought Lee was a threat or was about to take its prey, it might attack. He took a cautious step around the deer's corpse, cringing when a fallen twig snapped beneath his shoe. He froze, scanning the growing gloom about him for any sign of movement. But there was nothing. He took one last look at the bloody carcass and headed back toward the cabin.

The back of his neck prickled as he made his way down the trail. Everything – his vision, his hearing, even his sense of smell – seemed heightened and aroused as he imagined every tiny sound, every dark shadow to be the beast closing in on him. The dank perfume of the winter woods, mingled with the fishy smell of the lake and the odor of blood choked him, and just as his own boat dock appeared out of the mist, he doubled over and vomited a stream of hot, sour bile, holding tight to a sapling so he wouldn't fall. With one final glance behind him, he staggered up the hill and climbed the steps of the deck to the sliding doors.

Inside, the house was dark and cold. He passed through the dining room to the kitchen, flipping on lights as he went, and filled a glass with tap water. He drank it all without stopping, even when he momentarily gagged thinking about the dead deer and the smell emanating from its eviscerated body.

A bobcat. Had to be. He would need to be careful out here by himself. He'd heard they rarely attacked humans, but who knew what might happen if one got hungry enough. He would be dead before he got a chance to even get his cell phone out to call for help. Tomorrow he would find a good walking stick, maybe a sturdy limb, and start carrying it with him when he was outside. If he didn't have a gun he at least needed some way to defend himself, however meager it might be.

He rummaged through the freezer. He knew he needed to eat; he'd had nothing all day except that Pop Tart. But the idea of food turned his stomach. When he closed his eyes he could still see the deer's intestines splayed over the trail, could still smell the blood. He shuddered with revulsion and slammed the freezer door. Tonight he would opt for bourbon.

The overhead lights had become harsh and glaring, and he turned them off again as he wound through the house to the living room. In the sudden darkness, he caught a foot against a barstool and went sprawling across the floor, cracking his elbow against the hardwood. *"Fuck!"* He sat up, cradling his arm and bearing down as he waited for the pain to dissipate. He'd probably have a pretty nasty bruise there tomorrow, but he was lucky he hadn't hit his head.

He climbed to his feet, reaching out to steady himself on the bar, and his gaze caught on the patio doors for a moment, just long enough to see the shadow pass across in the dim light. The shock of the sudden movement sent him reeling backward again, but this time he caught himself before he could go down. Was it the bobcat? Had it followed him back to the cabin?

But no. The shadow had been too tall. It had been a person.

He slipped into the dining room toward the patio doors and peered into the settling darkness. The deck was empty, and the walkway lights trailed off into the dark mist. His hand flailed at the light switch and the deck was suddenly illuminated.

Nothing.

Lee slid the door open and stepped out into the twilight. The floodlights mounted to the house cocooned the deck against the darkness. Even if the fog hadn't been present he would not have been able to see more than a few feet over the edge. "Hello?" he called. "Who's there?"

He strained his ears for some slight sound – the breaking of a branch, the rustle of a leaf – but only dead silence answered him.

"I have a gun," he shouted, hoping the quiver in his voice didn't betray the fact he was lying. "Stay away or I'll shoot the fuck out of you."

He slammed the door to and turned the deadbolt, then flicked off the deck lights and watched the outside sink into inky darkness. He wished now he'd let Jessie hang some vertical blinds in here when she first asked instead of insisting on the view of the lake be left unobscured. It had been the one thing he'd refused to compromise on, but now they would make him feel less exposed to whatever might be out there looking in.

He set the alarm, then moved away from the door and back into the kitchen, switching on the undercabinet lights. Had he really said "I'll shoot the fuck out of you?" Good lord. Whoever was out there would probably laugh themselves to death.

He pulled out the Jim Beam and poured three fingers worth into a glass, then followed the glow of his laptop screen back to the dining room. The blank screen still mocked him, and he damned sure wasn't going to sit here facing the dark void beyond the patio doors when he couldn't see what was out there. And besides, who was he kidding? He would get no writing done tonight.

He closed the laptop and felt his way toward the living room, pausing to switch on the table lamp and the radio by the fireplace. The college station was playing light jazz tonight – Brubeck. He settled onto the sofa with his bourbon and picked up the Poe book, but laid it back on the coffee table when he remembered the dream from last night. He wasn't sure he wanted a repeat of that. His fingers idly played over his chest, rustling the bandage beneath his sweater, and he was relieved that the pain in the wound seemed to have left him.

He took a sip of the bourbon and let the warmth spread through him. It seemed like the only thing that could take away the chill that had settled into his bones since he got here. He'd forgotten to check the thermostat, but it seemed pointless. And Jessie had never called him back with the name of the HVAC guy they'd used before.

His phone buzzed. He reached for it on the side table and slipped on his reading glasses. A text message from a number he didn't recognize. *Hi Nicky.*

He shook his head. Obviously someone had misdialed. He texted back, *Sorry, I'm not Nicky. Wrong number.*

He dropped the phone on the sofa beside him and it immediately buzzed back to life. *Miss you.*

He blew out a breath and picked the phone back up. *You have the wrong number*, he tapped out.

A response flashed on the screen. *I'm cold.*

He stared at the words for a moment and felt a prickle along the back of his neck, and in spite of the bourbon, a chill passed through him.

The phone vibrated in his hand. *Come get me.*

This was getting irritating. Probably some drunken coed texting an old boyfriend. *For the last time, I'm not Nicky*, he wrote. *Stop texting me.* He set the phone down and blew out a breath. And just as he reached for his bourbon, the cell vibrated again, this time not with a text but with an incoming call. He looked at the display. The same number that had been texting. He gritted his teeth and answered it. "I told you to stop texting me. Don't call me, either. I'm not Nicky."

"I'm so cold, Nicky," the voice on the other end said. High and tearful and female. "Please come get me."

"If you need help, call nine-one-one," Lee told her. "But leave me the fuck alone."

"Nicky, am. . . am I *dead?*"

Horror washed over him and he disconnected the call, feeling both foolish and angry. He immediately tapped into the phone settings and blocked the number, then tossed the phone aside. Just a prank caller no doubt, probably dialing random numbers just to get a rise out of someone. Unless. . . unless it was connected to the shadow on the deck he'd seen earlier. Or the dead deer.

No. He refused to draw any kind of connection between all that. A bobcat killed that deer. The shadow he only imagined he'd seen. And the calls had come from some drunken fool trying play a joke. He was letting his imagination run away with him again, and scaring himself instead of channeling it into his writing.

He downed the bourbon in one gulp, relishing the burn through his sinuses and all the way down his gullet, and smacked the glass back on the table. Fuck it all. Fuck Jessie, and fuck the dying marriage he was locked into. Fuck writing. Fuck Bill and his goddamned deadlines. Fuck Circle. Fuck Max Plexico. Fuck old Mr. Saunders and his stories that had started his mind wandering in the first place. Fuck the fog and whatever had killed that deer. And fuck this goddamned cold house.

He snapped off the radio and trudged upstairs into the pitch black of the bedroom. It was colder up here if that was possible. He decided he'd take a hot shower, maybe relax on the couch and watch some TV. *The Walking Dead* was on tonight, and he wanted to catch up with whatever was happening with Rick's crew.

He pulled his sweater over his head and started the water, then carefully began the process of removing the bandage from the center of his chest. He managed to loosen the tape with only a minimum loss of chest hairs and then stared at the wound in the mirror.

Or where the wound had been.

His chest was completely unmarked. He ran his fingertips over the area, feeling for the puckered area that had bled profusely earlier but he could find nothing. It was smooth, as if the injury had never been there.

* * *

Once he'd showered and the bourbon had loosened him up, he decided to lie down and watch the TV in the bedroom. But as the opening scenes of *The Walking Dead* played out, he found himself struggling to follow the storyline as he dozed. And when he realized he'd missed half of the episode he turned off the television and let sleep take him over.

But his dreams were restless and disturbing.

He was back at the house in the city, climbing the stairs to the second floor. They had become shockingly narrow. He struggled to maneuver his grotesquely fat frame to the top. He knew with deep certainty that once he was up he would never come down again. Suddenly, Jessie appeared at the upstairs landing. She was dressed in black, a veil covering her face. She grasped something that was squealing, struggling to break free. It was Corey. "Stop! Stop!" Lee tried to scream, but his words only came out as a choked whisper. He watched, impotent, as Jessie lifted Corey high above her head and flung him over the rail. The boy hit bottom with a deep resounding thud. Lee stared, horrified, as blood began to pool around the body. And when he turned to look back at Jessie she had removed her veil, revealing her face to be a gory, maggot-ridden, smiling skull.

Lee jolted awake, his eyes searching the darkness for anything he could fix his vision on. He finally focused on the open door of the bedroom, and the glow of the table lamp from downstairs. There was just enough light to see the edge of the bed and the faint shadow of the chest across the room.

God, what a dream. Two nights in a row now he'd dreamed of Jessie. Dark, terrible dreams. He almost regretted throwing away the medication from Dr. Thayer.

He rolled over and closed his eyes, waiting for sleep to come again.

Then the gnawing started.

He opened his eyes and listened to it. And this time it wasn't just above his head. It seemed to come from everywhere and nowhere. It was all around him. In the walls, the ceiling. Under the floorboards. Gnawing and scratching and chewing.

"Go find the poison, you little fuckers," he called out.

He balled up under the covers and covered his head with his pillow. And soon, in spite of the incessant noise, he was back asleep.

III

Smoke

HE AWOKE TO A ROUND OF THUNDER shaking the house and rattling the windowpanes. The bedroom was awash in dim gray light. He lay with the blankets bunched about his neck and watched the rain droplets spatter against the window, then race one another down the glass. The clock on his phone read 9:03. He stretched, feeling the fatigue in his legs from the hike. God, he was out of shape.

The vision of the gutted deer swam before him, and he again wondered whether he had missed a hungry bobcat by mere moments. He would have to remember to ask Harvey if he'd seen any around. Lee wasn't easily spooked, but he had to admit that stumbling upon the deer's carcass in the twilight combined with the shadow on the deck and the unsettling series of anonymous text messages and odd call later at least had him feeling uneasy.

He pulled himself out of the bed and padded to the

bathroom. As he stood at the toilet he fingered the area on his chest where the wound had suddenly appeared and just as mysteriously vanished. It made no sense at all. Even the skin of victims suffering from stigmata held onto some evidence of trauma for days after the event. He shook his head and stepped into a pair of jeans, then pulled a sweatshirt over his head. He needed coffee and breakfast. He'd hardly eaten anything the day before and now he felt weak and shaky.

But first he wanted to check the bait in the attic. The gnawing he remembered waking to in the middle of the night had sounded like hundreds of mice had invaded the house. One lone rodent had multiplied into scores. In the hall closet he flipped on the light and slid open the trap door to the attic, then climbed atop the stool and stuck his head into the yawning black opening. He didn't have the flashlight, but enough light filtered up from below to illuminate the bar of mouse poison he'd left.

It hadn't been touched. No teeth marks, no claw marks, nothing. And no rodent droppings to indicate the nasty varmints had even been near it. Disgusted, he slid the cover closed and left the attic. Surely they would come across it sooner or later.

Downstairs he started a pot of coffee and as it brewed he watched the restless lake in the gray light. The fog was gone, but now the rain obscured the opposite shore. Again, the sense of isolation settled upon him, and the silence of the house save for the gurgle of the coffee maker pressed on him from all sides.

He wondered whether the bobcat had come back and finished with the deer or whether it had dragged the carcass off into the woods somewhere. Hopefully he wouldn't have to dispose of it himself. And then something struck him. At no point had he seen any animal tracks around the deer. Of course it had been dark, and he was a little freaked out, but still... Maybe he should go back and take a look.

But as he watched the rain pelt the glass of the patio doors, he knew he wouldn't go out there today. What would be the point? As hard as the rain was falling it had probably obliterated any leftover tracks anyway.

Today was Monday. Tomorrow morning was the call with Bill. He would have to come up with something before then. The days of putting off Bill and Circle were long gone. Circle had advanced him, what, fifty grand when he signed the new contract? So far he'd been paid half of it. He could call his accountant, move around some investments, and easily come up with twenty-five thousand to repay them. And the contract would be voided. Deadlines would disappear. The pressure would be off.

But then what?

The royalties from the sale of the film rights to Max Plexico alone would keep his family comfortable for years, not to mention his interest in toy sales, audiobooks, and all those other options. Circle wouldn't drop the Max Plexico line, and neither would Bill; it was too profitable for all of them. So when Bill threatened to sever their working relationship, Lee knew he was bluffing. There was no way in hell Bill or Circle would turn loose of the Max Plexico cash cow.

The coffee maker gave a final wheeze and Lee left the patio doors to pour a cup. But the aroma which usually gave him a surge of pleasure and anticipation revolted him. He took a small sip and his stomach clenched in disgust. He spat it out in the sink. The taste was foul. Bitter. Like dirt. God, was something wrong with the coffee? He flipped open the top of the brewer and stared down at the what lay in the filter.

Worms. Tiny, white worms. Curled up and dead atop the damp coffee grounds. Dozens of them.

With his finger he dug into the hot dregs, unearthing more of the little white bodies. They were all through the basket.

With growing horror he pulled off the plastic lid of the coffee can and peered into it. The coffee was crawling with them. They slithered through the dry grounds like miniscule snakes, their segmented bodies squirming and coiling as if in orgasmic spasms. Too long and thin to be maggots or grubs. Why hadn't he seen them before now? He'd been scooping coffee from the canister for a couple of days now. Had there been some kind of eggs in it that had hatched overnight? My God, he'd been drinking potfuls of the stuff and –

He bent over the sink, gagging. His empty stomach heaved involuntarily, doubling him over, and white spots flickered across his vision.

He was taking the canister back to Mr. Saunders. There would be no more coffee from there. Instead, he'd go into town, to the little grocery. And just to be on the safe side, he'd get a different brand.

He dumped the pot down the sink, covering his nose and mouth against the earthy odor, and rinsed the drain with hot water. The coffee maker would have to be thoroughly cleaned. His belly gave one more spasm, and he thought maybe it would be best to even just throw the damn thing away.

His head reeled, and he gripped the counter to keep from falling over. He was hungry. He'd hardly eaten anything since he'd been here, subsisting on bourbon and tainted coffee. He took a granola bar from the cabinet and forced himself to eat it, even though his mind and stomached rebelled at the idea of food. Still, it would keep him from passing out from low blood sugar.

He trudged upstairs for his wallet and keys. He would go right now and return the coffee, and while he was in town he'd stop by that waterfront café and get some breakfast. A real breakfast with eggs and bacon and toast. Maybe some hashbrowns. He was sick from lack of food and what he'd just found. That's what it was. He needed a decent meal and a worm-free cup of coffee.

He'd just reached the bottom of the stairs when a dull thump sounded against the patio doors. He immediately thought of the shadow he'd seen last night, and his heart leaped.

There was a shape at the bottom of the door. It was a long-haired tabby cat, drenched and pitiful. Not a kitten, but still fairly young from the looks of it. The thump came again, and Lee realized the poor thing was batting at the glass, trying to get his attention. Its gaze locked with his, and it let out a high-pitched, lonesome yowl.

Lee slid open the door and the cat stepped casually inside, as if it belonged there, and rubbed its face against Lee's jeans, purring loudly. Lee picked it up. It seemed to weigh nothing. He held it against his chest and the cat's body was wracked with shivering, the purring broken into rough spasms. "Oh, you poor baby," Lee said to it. "What are you doing out there?" It peered into his eyes, and he felt something loosen in his chest. "Let's get you dried off. You're soaked."

He carried the cat upstairs to the bathroom and wrapped it in a towel, soaking up the water as best he could. The cat purred and purred, its eyes half-closed and its paws kneading the towel.

"I see you're a girl," Lee said after he'd had a look under the cat's tail. He stroked the damp fur between her ears and the cat butted her head against his fingers. "I bet you're hungry. Where'd you come from, anyway?"

He carried her back downstairs and placed her gently on the kitchen floor, where she promptly began to groom. There wasn't much in the way of cat food here at the cabin, but he'd bought a few cans of tuna and that would have to do for the moment. He dumped the contents of one of the tins into a bowl and set it before her, and she immediately cut short her washing and dove into it, her purrs coming louder, if that were possible.

He sat cross-legged beside her, stroking her between the ears as she wolfed down the tuna. Even through her rough appearance he could tell she was a beautiful cat. She looked to be eight or nine months old, and her gray and white fur still had a soft, wispy, kittenish feel to it. Though her ribs weren't prominent, Lee was sure she hadn't eaten in days. She gobbled down the remaining bits of tuna in the bowl and went to washing her face and paws.

He could keep her, he thought. She would be a good companion in the midst of the isolation and quiet. And maybe she could help with the rodent problem since the damn things seemed too smart to eat the poison. And she wouldn't be like a dog that needed constant attending to. Or a person, who would talk and be a distraction to his writing.

But he would need a few supplies. Food, a litter box, a couple of toys... Kesterson's probably had those things, but maybe he would head over to Cedar Hill and go to one of the big pet stores. There would be more of a variety there. And besides, it would give him an excuse to get out of here and not do any writing. Anything to procrastinate.

He blew out a breath and gazed at the colorless light outside the patio doors. This retreat hadn't been about writing. Not really. He'd been deluding everyone, including himself. This had been about getting away from everyone and everything. Jessie, the kids, everything. He'd really just wanted to be alone for a while. Some time to do whatever the hell he wanted, even if he just wanted to do nothing. It hadn't been about, as he had told Jessie and everyone else, sparking his inspiration with a change of scenery. He had run away. He was hiding. He was tired of being Lee Houston. He was ready to walk in someone else's shoes for a while, to be anonymous. To be a normal man.

With that, he gave the cat one last stroke down her damp back, grabbed the canister of coffee off the counter, and headed out the front door.

The rain hit him with an icy blast, and by the time he reached the Escalade his shirt was wet and clinging to his skin, and he cursed himself for not snatching his jacket. He fired up the engine and sat shivering as he waited for the heat to kick in. And when at last he felt the air grow warmer, he turned the switch to the maximum and relished the hot blast across his cold flesh. It was the first time he'd actually felt warm in days.

Mr. Saunders took the coffee back without question, and was genuinely appalled at the sight of the worms wriggling through the grounds. "You can bet your ass every one of these cans is going back," he told Lee, sliding the refund across the counter. "Never had anything like this happen before."

"Don't worry about it," Lee said. "I know it's not your fault."

"Still," Mr. Saunders said, "it gives you a bad impression of my store."

"Not a big deal," Lee said, pocketing the money.

Mr. Saunders leaned across the counter. "Hey, how're you getting along down there?"

"Fine," Lee told him. "Pretty quiet so far."

"You stocked up for the big snow? Supposed to get nasty over the next couple of days. You remember what I told you, right?"

"Yeah, I'm ready," Lee said, feeling the irritation bubble up within him. He appreciated the concern, but he didn't want a damn sermon on survival skills every time he talked to the man. He turned to leave, but stopped. "Are there any bobcats in these woods around the lake?"

Mr. Saunders scratched his chin with the back of his hand. "Oh, yeah. Don't see much of 'em, except maybe a dead one on the highway ever' once in a while." He looked directly at Lee. "Why?"

Lee shrugged, almost afraid to voice his concern. "I. . . I think one got a deer close to my place. Found a carcass on the lake trail. It was pretty torn up."

Mr. Saunders nodded. "Yeah, they get hungry, just like everything else. Just be careful. Don't go walking around out there by yourself without your gun."

Lee forced a smile. "Sure."

"What'd you say you got? A Glock?"

"Yeah."

"What kind is it? Nine millimeter? Forty-five?"

Lee stiffened and his face burned hot. "Nine," he said. "Nine millimeter."

Mr. Saunders leaned across the counter, his eyes narrowing. "You don't really have a gun, do ya?"

Lee forced a laugh and threw his hands in the air. "Okay, yeah, you got me. I don't have one."

Mr. Saunders stroked his chin. "Get one. Today."

Lee gave him a puzzled smile, but Mr. Saunders didn't return it. "Seriously?"

"Don't stay out there another night without one."

"Sure," Lee said. He backed up toward the door. "I'm going into Cedar Hill this morning anyway."

"Revlett's Gun Shop on Donaldson Street," Mr. Saunders said, straightening up. "Ol' Gary will take care of ya. Tell him I sent you and he'll probably give you a discount."

"That'd be great," Lee said, reaching for the door. "Appreciate it."

"Lee? I'm serious."

Lee nodded, his flesh suddenly clammy. "Okay."

Outside, he sloshed through the puddles of the gravel lot to the Escalade and headed toward town. Maybe Mr. Saunders was right. Maybe he *did* need a gun. Back home in the city, he'd never felt the need for one, especially living in an exclusive gated community. Crime was unheard of in The Pines; and even in the event of an emergency, help would arrive in less than two minutes. But here. . . He eyed the forest on either side of the lonely stretch of highway as he descended the hill into the town. The cabin might as well be a hundred miles from anything. And he'd bet everything he had that all those guys that frequented the front porch at Kesterson's owned more than one firearm. They weren't stupid. They weren't going to live in the middle of nowhere without some form of protection.

The heavy rain made the drive to Cedar Hill treacherous. Several times he felt the Escalade hydroplane on the water ponding on the pavement, and each time he had to fight for control of the wheel. He slowed down to forty-five, and the sheets of rain hitting the windshield still prevented him from seeing more than a couple of feet in front of him, even with his wipers on high. He remembered a boy in his junior class in high school who had died instantly when the Nissan Sentra he was driving through a thunderstorm hit a pool of water on the interstate and hurtled into a bridge overpass. Lee had been cautious during rainy drives ever since, and they still made him uneasy.

After the solitude and relative emptiness of Harper's Lake, the bustling traffic of Cedar Hill was jarring, even though he was used to the far busier streets of Springfield. The rain, lack of food and caffeine, and the constant fatigue he couldn't shake had all combined to make him jittery and wired, and he found himself muttering curses at other drivers, even blaring his horn when a white-haired lady cut him off in a turning lane.

When he was finally parked in the lot of the pet store, he sat for a moment listening to the rain drum on the roof of the Escalade, watching people rush in and out of the automatic front doors through the downpour. And when he decided the rain wasn't going to let up, he hopped out and made a mad dash across the pavement, splashing into one deep cold puddle and soaking his foot through the canvas of his sneaker. Inside the door he shook the water off his clothes as best he could, but there was no help for his waterlogged shoe, and it squelched with each step as he grabbed a cart and made his way toward the cat care aisle. As bright and inviting as the store had looked from outside, the air was cold and damp and carried the smells of cedar and chemicals and urine. He shivered, and the shudder seemed to reach to his bones.

He quickly filled the cart with a litter box and some furry mice toys and had just wheeled up to grab a bag of Friskies when he saw Kat. And this time he knew he wasn't hallucinating. She was holding two cans of cat food, comparing them apparently, studying them with the same intensity he'd seen on her face when writing a poem. She hadn't changed much. The few lines time had placed on her face only added to her beauty, giving her a mature, womanly presence. Beneath her khaki raincoat she wore a Cedar Hill College sweatshirt and jeans, and her hair – still the same soft shade of light brown he remembered – was held back with a wide knitted band. He'd always liked her hair that way, and he remembered how when he'd tell her, she'd laugh and say he was gross, that she only wore those bands in her hair on the days she hadn't washed it. He realized she was much, much prettier than the woman he'd seen outside the school. How on earth had he mistaken her for this goddess that now stood a mere ten feet away?

He stared at her for what seemed an hour, feeling a

hollow ache in his chest, and before he could stop himself, he said, "Hello, Kat."

She looked up at him, catching her breath. "Lee?" She dropped one of the cans of cat food and stooped to retrieve it, her gaze never leaving his.

"What are you doing here?" he asked. "I thought you were on the west coast."

She took a deep breath. "Long story. I was in Seattle for several years. I'm going through a divorce right now and I needed to get away. Got a job in the English department here at the college."

"Doing what?"

"Teaching freshman comp."

"Hey," he said, "that's the – "

"The same thing you taught," she finished for him, smiling and rolling her eyes. "Yeah, I know. Life is weird like that." They looked at each other in awkward silence for a moment, and finally she said, "So how've you been?"

He nodded. "Great."

"Obviously," she said. "Max Plexico has been good to you, I'll bet."

He laughed. "Yeah, you could say that." He cleared his throat. "You finally put a book out yourself, I saw."

Kat shrugged. "Well, you know. Twenty years' worth of drivel published in journals and e-zines. Had to end up somewhere." She tossed the cat food into the cart and gripped the handle. "So how's your family?"

"Fine," he said. "We're all fine." And when she nodded, he said, "You have any kids?"

She shook her head. "Nope. Being married to a music producer that keeps weird hours isn't conducive to making babies."

He detected the sadness in her tone and said, "I'm sorry, I guess I shouldn't have asked that." He instinctively reached for her hand, but stopped himself before he touched her.

She waved him off. "It's all right." She glanced at her watch. "Well, I've got to be going. I don't have any classes on Mondays, and I usually head over to a little coffee shop with my laptop and try to get some writing in."

Lee's mouth was suddenly dry. "Want some company?"

She looked at him warily. "Lee. . . "

"Just to catch up."

"I don't know, Lee. I'm not sure that's a good idea."

"It's just coffee," he said.

She looked away from him and brushed a strand of hair off her face. "Fourth Street Coffee, across from the library. I'll meet you there."

* * *

By the time Lee was settled at his table in the coffee shop, he was already feeling guilty. Why, he didn't know. It was only coffee. Nothing else. But he knew if word got back to Jessie they had been seen together she would think otherwise. Especially now. But there was no denying that Kat was still part of him. As many years as it had been, as badly as she had hurt him, every part of him still ached to be with her. And with the deterioration of his and Jessie's relationship, Kat was easier to think about.

Just when he was beginning to think she wouldn't show, the door opened and Kat swept in like an unexpected breeze. He watched her order a large latte and wind her way toward him. "You didn't bring your laptop," he said.

She shrugged. "What's the point?" She set her cup down and draped her wet raincoat over the back of a chair. She melted into the seat and blew onto her coffee. "I haven't written anything in months. Ever since the divorce started." She took a tentative sip. "I'm sure you wouldn't know anything about that."

He stared at the table. "About divorce or writer's block?"

"Either." She looked at him, then pushed her cup away. "Look, I knew this wasn't a good idea." She scooted her chair back and started to rise. "Let's just forget we did this."

Before he could stop himself, he reached out and grabbed her hand. "Please don't go." She glanced at the front door and he squeezed harder. "Please."

Kat sat back down. "What's wrong with you?" she hissed, but she left her hand in his.

He looked at the steam rising from his coffee. "Things just aren't going well." His eyes stung, but he was not going to cry. Not in front of Kat.

"What's the matter?" She moved her face closer to his. "Are you okay?"

He took a deep breath and shook his head. "I don't know. I don't know anything anymore." He looked into her eyes. "I know I shouldn't be here. *We* shouldn't be here."

She reached for her coat. "That's what I thought. I told you – "

"I've missed you, Kat."

"Don't do this, Lee."

"I think I still love you."

Kat looked toward the bearded man typing away at the next table, then back at Lee, her face blossoming red. "Stop it," she said in a harsh whisper. She leaned toward him and pulled her hand from his grasp. "What do you want from me?" She took a deep breath. "You ripped my heart out once. You are not going to do it again." She brushed the hair from her face. "You got everything you ever wanted. Two kids, a fine wife. I've seen pictures of your house on the internet. You got rich off your writing. You've got millions of fans. What more do you want?" Her eyes were shining now, and he realized she was crying. "It hasn't been easy for me, you know. Watching you over the years. Seeing your name everywhere. I can't go anywhere without seeing that goddamned Max Plexico." She wiped her eyes on her shirt sleeve. "And every time I see a picture of you and your wife, all I can think is that I should be her. That should be *me*." She looked away, sniffling. "Sorry, I shouldn't have said that."

He reached out and took her hands in his again. "We really fucked each other over good, didn't we?" He laughed and so did she.

"Yep." She dug a tissue out of her coat pocket and wiped her face. "I'm sorry. I had everything planned that I would say to you if I ever got to talk to you again. None of that was it."

"I've kept up with you, too, you know," Lee said. "The internet is a glorious thing. That's how I knew your book was coming out. I pre-ordered it months in advance."

She dabbed at the corners of her eyes. "Thanks for being one of the twelve people that actually bought a copy."

"I recognized a couple of those poems from when we were together."

She looked into her coffee, then took a small sip. "I guess you recognized yourself in 'Making Love on Sunday Morning.'"

He stared at her. "You wrote that about me?"

"You didn't notice?"

"I assumed it was about your husband."

She grunted. "So did he."

"I'll have to read it again."

They drifted into an uncomfortable silence. Lee took a sip of his coffee, grateful for the rich, bold flavor, and Kat traced a pattern on the table with her finger. Beside them, the bearded man drained his cup and closed his laptop. He glanced at them as he left his table, and Lee noticed the faint glimmer of recognition in his eyes. At one time being noticed in a public setting was flattering; now it was just creepy. The man stepped out onto the sidewalk and gave Lee one last stare through the front window before he disappeared into the rain.

Lee looked back at Kat. He cupped her hand in his, marveling at how much smaller hers were than Jessie's. "Look," he said, "I'll be honest. My life is going to shit. I haven't written anything in over a year. I've stopped answering the phone when my agent calls because I know he's going to want to see something and I've got nothing to show him. Jessie and I – well, we haven't slept in the same room for months. I guess you could say we're sort of separated. I'm staying at the lake house right now. I went down there to write, but. . . I think my marriage is about over."

"I'm sorry, Lee."

"I don't know what I'm doing anymore," he said.

"Nothing in my life has turned out like I thought it would. Nothing. This is not what I wanted, not at all. And when I saw you in the pet store it was like I was twenty-two again, like we had never been apart. Like my time with Jessie and writing all those books had just been a dream. And then you looked at me and – "

Without warning, Kat leaned across the table and kissed him on the lips. Long and slow. And everything in him melted.

* * *

They left the coffee shop with an exchange of numbers and the promise they would stay in touch. He drove back to Harper's Lake without any notice of the rain, and halfway there he realized a grin was plastered on his face. There was a feeling in his gut, warm and fluttery, that he hadn't felt in years, and it had Kat written all over it. He felt *alive*. Awake. As if he had been sedated and just blazed into consciousness. It was the same feeling he remembered from falling in love with Kat in college, giddiness and terror and horniness all rolled together.

But at the same time, his joy was tempered with guilt. He and Jessie were still married after all. And although they hadn't been intimate in months, he couldn't think about Kat without his moral compass trying to rein him in. He wondered how he would feel if the situation were reversed, if it were Jessie who had met an old lover for coffee and was now feeling sexually charged from the encounter. And he realized that he wouldn't care. That if he discovered she had been dallying with someone outside their marriage it would be a relief. That he would have an excuse to end their relationship once and for all and not feel remorseful about it. It was a hell of a thing to realize, that your marriage had deteriorated to the point where you were completely dispassionate about your spouse. And yet, here he was.

The rain had let up by the time he reached the cabin, though the air had turned chilly, and for once the inside of the house felt warm. He unloaded his purchases just inside the doorway and looked about for the cat. There was a moment of panic when he couldn't locate her downstairs, but he finally discovered her curled up in a fluffy gray ball on the foot of his bed. She opened her eyes when she sensed him in the room and turned her head to look at him, stretching out a paw toward him and yawning.

"Found the most comfortable spot in the house, I see," Lee said. He picked her up and carried her down to the living room. "I got some things for you."

He fastened the new collar around her neck – pink with paw print-shaped rhinestones – and opened the pack of mouse toys, and while she was occupied with those he set up the litter box just inside the laundry room. He sat and watched her for a few minutes as she batted the mice across the floor and romped around the furniture. He had forgotten how entertaining kittens could be.

He had picked up a new can of coffee on his way through town, bypassing Saunders', and when he opened it, he was relieved to see only ground coffee in the canister. No worms. He fixed a pot and while it brewed he showed the kitten the new litter box, then watched her scramble after the toy mice some more. She was certainly enjoying them, but he knew before the day was done he'd be digging all of them out from under the furniture.

When the coffee was done, he poured a cup and sniffed it. The aroma was rich and bold. So far, so good. He took a small sip, and was relieved to discover the flavor was normal. He hoped whatever had been in the previous container hadn't come from inside the cabinet, but he double-checked the seal on the lid just to make himself feel better.

In the living room, he dug around the bookshelf until he found Kat's book, squeezed between an old Evan Hunter novel and a battered paperback copy of *The Hobbit*. He pulled it out, blowing dust off the top, and ran his fingertips over the glossy cover – a minimalist painting of a lake in the mountains. *Blue Waters: Poems by Kat Cunningham.* He thumbed through the slim volume until he found "Making Love on Sunday Morning." He skimmed it, searching for any likeness of himself. It was vague and meandering, and reminded him of why he'd never enjoyed Kat's poetry. It was all disjointed thoughts that never reached any kind of conclusion, random observations of meaningless minutiae. For all the blurbs of praise emblazoned on the cover, he couldn't for the life of him imagine why anyone thought any of her work was worthy of publication. "Sunday Morning" gave him no feeling at all; it was lifeless and flat, and if it were any reflection of Kat's perception of their lovemaking, theirs had been a sorry relationship indeed. He shelved the book with an odd sense of disappointment. Seeing Kat again had stirred up old emotions good and bad, and for a brief moment he'd felt the bittersweet pang of college days. But now it all seemed as pretentious as one of Kat's poems. As hollow and fake as a stage set.

Outside, the rain had all but stopped. From where he stood at the patio door he could once again see the town across the water in the distance and the traffic flowing smoothly down Lake Shore Drive. Business as usual.

The rain had agitated the lake, and the water was black and roiling under a slate-colored sky. He sipped at his coffee and watched it lap at the shore and smack against the dock. Across the chaotic waves, a fishing boat bobbed in the center of the lake, its lone occupant clad in a yellow rain slicker, and Lee wondered why the hell anyone would be out in the middle of a downpour. Unless it was some guy trying get away from his wife for a while, and he chuckled at that thought. "More power to ya, bud," he whispered, raising his cup in a mock toast.

He was just turning away from the window when something at the edge of the dock caught his eye, gray and drifting in the dark water, knocking against one of the weathered pilings. He stared in horror. It was a hand. Reaching. The arm it was attached to stretched down into the murk. While his brain tried to comprehend what his eyes were seeing, what he knew wasn't – *couldn't* – be there, the fingers moved. The hand clenched into a fist and opened again.

Lee's coffee cup fell to the tile floor with a crash. Coffee and stoneware fragments exploded in all directions.

He swung the patio door open and flew across the deck toward the steps. But the rain had slickened the wood and he went tumbling down to the bottom, landing in a heap on the pea-gravel walkway. He sat up, stunned. He was in a puddle, and his jeans were already soaked through. He clamored to his feet, vaguely aware of a sharp pain in his back, and raced down the slope toward the dock, toward whomever needed help. They wouldn't last any time in the frigid water.

He reached the water's edge and stopped. What he'd thought was a beckoning hand was only a tree branch drifting in the rough current. It banged and clawed against the side of the dock, and now that he was just a few feet from it, he wondered how the hell he ever could have mistaken it for anything human.

He rubbed his eyes, suddenly feeling very foolish and very tired.

Back at the cabin he changed out of his wet clothes and into sweats. A painful bruise was already blossoming just beneath his shoulder blade, and he hoped he hadn't cracked a rib in his fall. While his shirt was off, he examined the center of his chest again, amazed there was no sign of his earlier wound. If the blood stains weren't still on his clothes, he would think he'd hallucinated that, too. He pulled on a t-shirt and made his way back downstairs.

The kitten was curled in front of the fireplace, chewing on the tail of a purple mouse. She watched him as he made his way through the room, her mouth continuing to work on the strip of fur. "That's right," he told her. "Get some practice on those so you can go after the real ones around here."

He pulled a broom from its place in the corner and started toward the shards of the shattered cup, but before he could grab the paper towels to sop up the puddle of coffee, there was a knock on the front door.

For an insane moment, he wondered if it could be Kat, that maybe she had followed him back from Cedar

Hill and wanted to continue their conversation from the coffee shop. That she had felt the same rekindling of their love he had and wanted to start over. His heart leaped in his chest. He flung the broom to the side and practically floated toward the front door and threw it open.

Harvey stood there, his hands in the pockets of his overalls. "Well now," he said, "that's the most disappointed face I've seen since the first night Gail saw me take off my boxer shorts."

Lee laughed, and stepped aside to let the man in. "What're you doing out in this shitty weather?"

"Daily walk," Harvey said. "Thought I'd drop in." He spotted the cat and nodded at her. "See you found a friend."

Lee nodded. "Yeah, she showed up at the back door this morning, drenched to the bone." He looked at Harvey. "Know anybody that's missing a cat?"

Harvey shook his head. "Nope. 'Course I haven't talked to nobody except you."

"Just as well, I guess," Lee said. "I've got mice. Hordes of 'em from the racket I've been hearing. Hope she's a good mouser."

"Lucky she found you, before a coyote or something got to her."

Lee stroked the stubble on his chin. "Or a bobcat."

Harvey nodded. "Yeah. Everything gets hungry this time of year." He cleared his throat and looked back at Lee. "Do I smell coffee?"

"Just made a pot. Come on in." He led Harvey back to the kitchen. "Help yourself. You know where the mugs are."

Harvey pointed at the broom. "Did I catch you doing

housework?"

Lee shook his head. "Cleaning up a mess." He grabbed the paper towels and began blotting up the coffee. "I was standing here while ago and thought I saw. . . " He trailed off, not sure he wanted to continue his thought. What would Harvey think if he knew Lee was seeing things?

Harvey topped off a mug with coffee and turned toward him. "Saw what?"

Lee blew out a breath. "I thought I saw somebody down there in the water. Thought they were in trouble." He felt his face growing hot. "It was just a tree branch."

Harvey nodded and grinned. "Spooked you, huh?"

"Startled me is all," Lee said. He soaked up the remaining coffee and gathered some of the larger pieces of the cup into the paper towels.

Harvey blew on his coffee and took a sip. "Well, it happens. I tell ya, it's being out here by yourself. You see things. You hear things." He looked at Lee squarely. "You *imagine* things."

Lee thought of what all he'd experienced since he'd been in the cabin – the gnawing sounds, the figure on the deck. The wound in the center of his chest. "Yeah, I suppose so," he said. He swept the remnants of the cup into the dust bin and deposited them into the trash. Was Harvey right? Had all those things just been in his head? But that still didn't explain the blood on his shirts, the worms in the coffee. The bizarre text and call last night.

Harvey set his cup down on the bar. "You've only been out here, what, a couple of days? You're gonna be a basket case if you stay out here all winter long."

Lee grunted and pulled another cup from the cabinet.

"Hope not," he said, filling it.

Harvey nodded. "Well don't stay cooped up in here day and night, at least not while the weather's holding out. Go to town and grab dinner at The Sail. Go over to Cedar Hill and catch a movie. Hell, come up to my place one night and we'll play cards. Texas Hold-'em. You like poker?"

Lee chuckled. "Haven't played since college. And usually there was beer involved."

Harvey laughed loudly, smacking the bar and making Lee jump. "Well, we will have beer. And cigars."

Lee leaned back against the counter, cradling the coffee cup in his hands. "I guess it's everything, just playing with my mind. All the shit going on with my marriage, trying to write. Just getting to me. Found a dead deer down there on the lake trail last night, all torn up. And I got some weird texts and phone calls last night. I'm just. . . unnerved." He told Harvey about his trek to the Millers' and how the deer had been killed and mutilated during the time he had passed the lookout and returned. "Figured it was a bobcat. Mr. Saunders said there's some down here."

Harvey nodded. "Oh, yeah. You ever hear one of 'em scream? Sounds just like a woman. Horrible. And in the winter you can hear them clear on the other side of the lake. That screaming. . . coming across the water like that." He shivered. "They'll come clear up to your house sometimes. Found one sleeping on my back porch once."

Lee thought of the shadow he'd seen on the deck and felt oddly relieved. "Good to know," he said. "You'd think they'd steer clear of people."

"Mostly they do," Harvey said. "But you never know what a wild animal will do when it gets hungry. Or horny. It's close to their mating season. You're liable to hear a ruckus if two of 'em get into it." He set his cup down. "So what kinda calls were you getting last night?"

Lee waved a dismissing hand. "Oh, nothing really. Just a wrong number. Or a prank. Started out with a couple of texts. Some girl looking for somebody named Nicky. Then she started calling. I finally just blocked her." He glanced at Harvey and noticed the man's face was ashen. "You all right?"

Harvey smiled faintly. "Oh, yeah, sorry. The name just kinda threw me. Had a son named Nicky."

"Oh, really?"

Harvey nodded and sipped his coffee. "Yeah. He passed away back in 'ninety-one."

"Oh, I'm sorry to hear that. What happened?"

Harvey took a deep breath and stared out the patio doors, toward the dark water. "Drowned. Right out there in the lake."

Lee felt a sudden wave of sympathy for the man. He tried to imagine losing Corey or Lizbeth and found the idea simply too horrible to comprehend. He wanted to ask Harvey how it happened, but he was afraid of sounding ghoulish, like someone slowing down to stare at a highway accident.

But Harvey continued to talk anyway, keeping his gaze on the lake. "He and his girlfriend took our little fishing boat out one Sunday afternoon. It was in the middle of the summer, and it was hot there at the house. Nicky said they were going over to a cove on the south side of the lake where the water was cooler. They were gonna swim, meet some friends. Probably have a party. I mean, I'm not stupid, I knew what they were up to. But hell, all those kids were in their twenties, so it wasn't like they were teenagers or anything. Nicky was responsible. He'd just finished college and started a paid internship with a big accounting firm in St. Louis. Carly, his girlfriend, she was going to start med school that fall. Both of 'em smart kids." Harvey trailed off and sipped his coffee.

Lee waited a moment, then said, "So what happened?"

"Squall came up out of the blue. One of those big powerful summer storms. Wind and lightning and hail. Gail and I didn't get too worried until after sunset, when they didn't come back home. We figured they'd all holed up at the cove to let it pass. I made a few calls and found out when the weather started getting bad Nicky and Carly decided to leave the rest of 'em and head back home. They must've got caught in the worst of it. Nicky was a strong swimmer, but he would've been no match for the water that day. I don't remember ever seeing it that stirred up before. The water patrol started looking for them that night. Found the boat capsized and drifting in the middle of the lake. Nicky's body washed ashore the next morning."

"That's terrible," Lee said. "I'm so sorry."

"Carly. . . well, they never did find her. Everybody held out hope for a couple of days, thinking she might have made it to shore and got lost in the woods. People searched for her but they never found a trace. Coast Guard came and dragged the lake for a week, looking for her. Nothing."

"Did they send divers down or anything?"

"The problem is the lake depth. Deepest lake in this part of the country. Out in the center it's close to seven hundred feet deep. The water stays frigid down there, even in the hottest part of the summer. Once bodies go down in the middle of the lake, they don't usually come back up. They don't decompose like they do in the shallower water, so they don't float."

Lee shook his head. "I had no idea. . . ."

"A year after the accident some little kid on the public beach found something at the water's edge. Turned out to be the top of Carly's bathing suit. How or why it resurfaced after all that time nobody could say."

"That must have been really hard for her parents." He looked at Harvey. "For all of you."

Harvey nodded. "It was a rough time. Officially, Carly's still listed as a missing person since her body was never found, but we all know she's dead." He chuckled humorlessly. "I guess the strangest thing about it is where they finally found Nicky's body."

"Where was that?"

"Right down there." Harvey pointed out the patio doors. "Right at the edge of your dock."

* * *

After Harvey left, Lee sat at the dining table, staring out at the gray restless water and trying to push the image of the reaching hand from his mind. It had been so vivid and so real. The gray fingers clenching and stretching, reaching for the edge of the dock. The arm disappearing into the dark water, attached to something Lee couldn't begin to imagine, something slimy and putrid and long dead. And he wondered whether what he remembered seeing was actually as he had witnessed it, or if his memory had been clouded by Harvey's story.

Nicky, am I dead?

He shivered violently and took a sip of his lukewarm coffee. God, it was cold in here again. He trudged upstairs and grabbed a sweatshirt, pulling it over his head as he came back down to the living room. The cat was curled up on the sofa, purring loudly in her sleep, one paw draped over a toy mouse. He was glad he'd taken her in, and he hoped she would make a good companion.

His gaze fell on his phone on the coffee table. He reached for it and thumbed back through the text conversation with the unknown number. The girl's voice, pleading and tearful, wormed through his mind.

I'm so cold, Nicky.

And Harvey's story.

Carly. . . well, they never did find her.

Lee opened the detail window of the text and unblocked the number, and before he could stop himself he hit the call button, feeling his heart quickening in his chest. He waited for the call to connect, thinking he had no idea what he would say if the voice on the other end picked up. But no one answered. After ten rings he disconnected the call. He'd not even been able to get through to any sort of voice mail.

Once bodies go down in the middle of the lake, they don't usually come back up.

He opened the text window and stared at it for a moment, wondering whether he should send a message. Did he really want to get into another bizarre conversation with someone who was obviously just fucking around with him? He punched in *Did you ever find Nicky?* and hit "Send." He waited for a response, but his message just sat in the text window until the screen darkened and turned off.

He sank onto the sofa beside the sleeping cat and closed his eyes. The morning had wiped him out, and he found himself nodding off, lulled by the silence and dim light in the house.

A noise jolted him awake, and as he opened his eyes he realized it had been his phone vibrating with an incoming message. He glanced at the screen, expecting another crazy text from whomever he'd been talking with. Instead it was a text from Kat. *Hey.*

Hey yourself. What's up? he wrote back.

After a long pause, during which Lee wondered if Kat was going to answer or if she had lost her nerve, the phone buzzed. *Thinking about our conversation today and hoping I didn't come off as psycho.*

He smiled. *You're not psycho. It was good to see you.*

The phone sat silent and still for a few minutes. And just when he thought the conversation was over, a message flashed on the screen. *Dinner tonight?*

He stared at the text, thinking of how she'd kissed him in the coffee shop. How her lips, soft and warm, had tasted of coffee and cinnamon, and how her eyes had closed just before his mouth met hers. How seeing her, touching her, *smelling* her had jolted through him like something electric and alive.

His thumbs flew over the screen: *Yes.*

* * *

The restaurant was a tiny steakhouse just on the outskirts of Cedar Hill, a worn-looking white cinderblock building with an ancient neon sign and a reputation of serving the best steaks in the state, a place he'd occasionally brought Jessie while they were dating when he'd had the extra funds to splurge. Lee rolled into the gravel parking lot and found Kat waiting for him already, sitting snugly in her red Beetle. A pang of longing hit him. She waved and stepped out. Lee cut the engine and slid out of the Escalade, surprised at how sharp and bitter the air had become. "It got cold," he said, shivering in the light sports jacket he'd worn. He bent toward her and gave her an awkward kiss on the cheek.

"Let's get inside," she said. "It's freezing out here and I need a drink."

Inside, the aroma off the grill made his stomach growl, and he realized he'd barely eaten anything the past two days. It would be good to get a nice meal. The hostess, a short blonde who appeared as though she was barely out of high school, led them through the dim interior to a quiet booth in the corner and left them with a pair of grease-stained menus.

"So what's good here?" Kat said, looking over the selections.

"Haven't been here in years," Lee said, "but I never got a bad meal once. It's all good." He pulled his reading glasses out of his jacket pocket and slipped them on. He glanced up to see Kat watching him, smiling. "What?"

"I was just thinking how nice those look on you. You look. . . *mature*."

"I *am* mature," he said. "Hell, I'll be forty this year."

"You look good," she said, her voice tinged with sadness. "You look like a man. Not a boy any longer."

He smiled and felt his face flush. "You're still lovely as ever." He reached across the table and took her hand, squeezed it. She squeezed back, and he felt a warmth spread through him. Again his mind filled with things he wanted to tell her, confessions of lying in bed next to Jessie on sleepless nights while guiltily remembering making love to Kat, daydreaming about her endlessly sometimes instead of writing when he sat in front of his computer screen. Wondering how differently life would have turned out if they'd just tried a little harder to make things work out. But none of that seemed to make it to his lips, and the two of them sat in heavy silence, stealing glances at each other over the tops of their menus and grinning when they caught themselves.

They ordered drinks. Kat got an amaretto sour – the same thing she used to get when they were together, and he wondered how many other things about her had remained the same. He ordered a Fat Tire, and as he poured it carefully into his glass to minimize the foaming, his gaze lit on Kat's hands, and the ring he'd given her all those years ago. The inexpensive ruby surrounded by cubic zirconias. She was still wearing it. After all this time.

"Look out!" Kat cried, and he realized he'd missed the glass and poured beer across the table.

He grabbed his napkin and blotted up the mess, feeling his face grow hot. "God, what a klutz."

Kat giggled behind her hand. "Same old Lee," she said.

He wadded the soaked napkin and pushed it to the

side. "That ring," he said, pointing. "You kept it."

She looked at it and smiled, then met his gaze briefly before looking away. "I did."

He felt a grin playing on his lips. "Why?"

She held her hand out and watched it as she wiggled her fingers. "I thought it was pretty." She looked at him. "And the guy that gave it to me? I loved him very much."

He reached out and squeezed her hand again. "Do you ever wonder. . . ?"

"All the time," she said, pulling her hand away. "And then I tell myself that supposedly things happen for a reason, that somehow something in the cosmos – God, or whatever – knew we shouldn't be together."

"That's bullshit," he said. "We just didn't try hard enough." He took a sip of his beer. "I still think sometimes that maybe I shouldn't have taken that teaching job, that I should have stayed up there with you."

She laughed, and there was no trace of humor in the sound. "And I still think sometimes that I should have followed you. Changed my major to something more practical like law or finance. Would've made my parents happier, too."

Lee took a deep breath and leaned back in the booth. "How *are* George and Jean?"

She took a sip of her drink. "Dead."

A jolt shot through him. "I'm sorry to hear that. Truly."

She shrugged. "We weren't close anymore after I moved to Seattle with Mike. Saw them maybe once a year on Christmas. Called them on birthdays. That was about it. They didn't approve of what they perceived as a 'gratuitous' lifestyle."

He looked at her. "Meaning. . . ?"

"Meaning they thought Mike and I were having drug-infused orgies every weekend with Prince and Madonna, I suppose. And it wasn't like that at all. Mike was producing demos for local bands, hardly making any money. Camping out in small clubs every weekend to check out up and coming musicians. Helping us make ends meet by teaching guitar lessons on the side. And I was doing my part by teaching freshman English at an all-girls high school, entering an occasional poetry slam. Sometimes winning, most times not. It really wasn't a very glamorous life."

"But things got better, right?" Lee said.

"Not really." She swirled her glass and took a sip. "Mike finally got one band's demo into the hands of some bigshot in L.A. Ever hear of a band called Crystal Marine?"

"No," he said. "I don't keep up with much new music anymore."

"Kind of alternative folk rock."

"I'm sure my daughter knows them."

"They got signed by RCA. Mike flew down for six weeks and worked with them on the new album. And they caught on like gangbusters. He made a shitload of money in a short amount of time. And when he came back to Seattle he had a cocaine habit and a case of herpes."

Lee gaped at her. "Holy shit."

"Yeah. Holy shit is right." She took a deep breath. "I couldn't stay with him. I moved out not long after that and tried to make it on my own. But Seattle's an expensive place to live, especially on a teacher's salary.

By then Mom and Dad had both passed away, and my brother and sister had their own careers and families and no room for a down-and-out sibling to take in. So I did the most logical thing I could think of. I started looking for jobs back east, back closer to home."

"So how long have you been back?"

"Since last summer. I got the call from the college in June, moved here the first of August."

Lee shook his head. "What a wild ride."

"Yeah. So I'm sorry if I seem a bit. . . defensive. I'm just still trying to figure things out."

"It's all right," he told her. "I've been trying to figure things out for a long time. Haven't got very far."

Kat ran a fingertip around the edge of her glass. "I don't mean to pry, but. . . "

"What?"

"How long have things been going bad with your wife?"

"A while," he said. "Shit, I don't know if they were ever *great*. It's like we found each other and just latched on, like two people clinging to a life raft. We were what each other needed at the time, I suppose."

She sipped her drink. "And now?"

He shook his head and stared at the drying foam on the inside of his glass. "I don't know. I still love her, but. . . "

"But what?"

He looked at her, into those deep dark liquid eyes of hers. "She's not you."

* * *

When dinner was over, he followed her back to her apartment near the campus, and before she could shut the door behind them, their lips were pressed together and she was once again in his arms. Her keys and purse fell to the hardwood floor with a clash, sending her white ghost-like Persian cat scurrying for cover, and her hands clutched at his face and hair, pulling him closer with a frantic need. She tasted of almond liqueur and the chocolate raspberry cake they'd shared for dessert, and he found himself devouring her as if she were a rare delicacy.

Kat led him to the bedroom and pulled him down into the unmade bed. His fingers twisted through her thick hair while he nuzzled her neck and pressed himself against her. She fumbled with the buttons of his shirt, and her hands found the bare flesh of his chest and stroked it. And suddenly she was naked, and he was struggling to free himself from his jeans. He had barely pulled them below his buttocks when she pulled him over onto her. She was wet and slick, and he entered her in one fluid motion, moving with her in unrelenting rhythm, his open shirt draping over them both, the denim of his jeans grinding the back of his thighs. She was moaning and sighing, her hips bucking in cadence to his thrusts. And then he could feel himself slipping over the edge and he was powerless to hold back. He grabbed onto her as the waves of pleasure hit him, and fifteen years of need and longing and desperation blasted out of him.

"I'm sorry," he whispered, struggling to catch his breath. "I didn't mean to – "

"Finish me, Lee," she said, her voice husky and pleading. She pushed his head down past her breasts, and his stubbled chin scratched across the smooth skin of her stomach. "Please."

He knelt between her thighs, drunk on the scent of their lovemaking, and plunged his tongue into her, tasting her, tasting his own seed, suckling on her clitoris, feeling the warmth of their combined fluids smear across his cheeks, feeling her thrust against him. She cried out, and her hands found his head and pressed him farther into her, her fingers curled tightly around his hair. And suddenly her breath became shallow and rapid and she stiffened, and he felt her pulsing against his tongue. She gave one final gasp, then fell limp.

Lee kissed her inner thigh, and moved upward, grazing his lips across her belly, across her nipples, and finally to her lips. She kissed him, her fingertips tracing a line from his jaw down across his shoulder. Her hand took his and moved it downward, pressing his fingers into her, then drew them back up to her face. She kissed the wetness on his fingertips, then took his fingers into her mouth one by one, looking him in the eyes as she did so. He kissed her again, then sank back onto the bed.

But his penis stayed stiff and throbbing. Kat traced up and down it with her fingers, and suddenly she hovered above him, taking him into her mouth. Her lips were hot, and her tongue swirled around him, and in spite of having just come, he felt another orgasm building up within him. And when it hit, searing and blinding, she kept her mouth on him until the last drops spurted out, then moved upward to place her lips on his, letting the thick fluid trickle from her mouth to his. He swallowed, feeling somehow he should be sickened by it but unable to deny the electric charge it gave him. She lay back in the crook of his arm and snuggled against him, twirling her fingers through the hair on his chest.

He lay there in the darkness, staring up into the black void where he knew the ceiling must be, wondering at the feel of the woman beside him that wasn't Jessie. Knowing he should be ashamed. Knowing he should feel guilty lying there with his jeans still open and twisted around his thighs, his shirt half-off and wadded beneath him. But he felt neither of those things. As the silence lingered and Kat began to snore softly, he realized how much he had missed her, how much of the past fifteen years had been wasted with a woman he thought he loved but now realized he didn't. A woman he had never really loved. A woman who apparently didn't love him either. A sadness washed over him as he thought of the time he and Kat had been apart, of all they had missed without each other.

He placed a kiss on her forehead, softly so as not to wake her, then nuzzled against her and let sleep overtake him.

* * *

When he awoke, the room was freezing and black as pitch, and he realized he was still lying half-naked on top of the bed. Kat lay beside him, facing away but still snuggled against him, the comforter wrapped around her. A glance at her alarm clock told him it was a little past one. His bladder was near bursting, and he tried to remember whether he'd seen a bathroom when they had come in earlier. He eased off the bed, pulling up his jeans and fastening the top button, then shuffled through the room toward the door. His shoulder smacked into a tall chest, and he heard something small fall over with a clatter. Kat stirred in her sleep and mumbled something, then resumed snoring.

He felt his way through the door and down the hallway and by some miracle found the bathroom. He squinted at the sudden brightness as he flipped the light switch and stood over the toilet, pissing silently against the side of the bowl and feeling the relief as his bladder emptied. He rinsed his hands in the sink and was just about to turn out the light when something on the vanity caught his eye. Four prescription bottles. He picked one up and read the label. Valium. The other three held Xanax, Ativan, and Percocet. All had Kat's name on the labels. All were dated just before Christmas. He looked at the four bottles all in a row, feeling numb. Jesus Christ. Kat hadn't lied when she said she was trying to figure things out.

He left the light on, intending on using it to find his way back to the bedroom, but he instead found himself in her living room. The white cat lay in a heap on an overstuffed chair, and he traced his fingers along its back, feeling it arch against his hand. The streetlamps outside cast an orange glow through the sheer curtains over the windows, and movement drew him closer. It was snowing, large flakes that were coming down furiously. The street and cars below were already covered. As he watched, a snowplow slipped past, silent as the snow itself, its yellow warning lights flashing blindingly across the blanket of white.

"What're you doing?" Kat stood in the hallway, silhouetted by the light from the bathroom. The comforter was wrapped around her like a robe.

"I got up to pee," he said. "It's snowing."

"Is it?" She moved toward him, taking tiny steps like a geisha, her legs bound by the cover. She peered through the curtains. "Wow. Looks like there's already a couple of inches out there."

"I better go," he said. "Before I get stranded and can't get back to Harper's Lake."

"Stay here," she said. "Get snowed in with me. It'll be fun." She pressed against him. "We can snuggle in bed all day. Make love, then nap. Then make love again." She smiled and he bent down to kiss her. She pulled back and he could see tears welling in her eyes. "You know today in the coffee shop when you said you'd missed me?"

"Yes."

"I've missed you, too." She laid her head against his shoulder. "I don't think I realized until now just how much."

He held her close and watched the snow fall, resting his head atop hers.

■ ■ ■

Though the plows had kept the streets relatively clear in town, the highway to Harper's Lake looked as though it had barely been touched. Something – a large truck from the looks of it – had left two black ruts through the slush, and he guided the Escalade carefully through the track. But the path was disappearing quickly in the heavy snow, and Lee wondered whether he had been a fool to leave the warmth and safety of Kat's apartment. With the four-wheel-drive engaged he was able to keep all the tires on the road, but as the previous driver's trail petered out, the challenge became discerning what was road and what was not. Several times he heard the crunch of gravel as he drifted off the pavement, and in each instance he struggled against the instinct to jerk the steering wheel to the left to avoid the ditch. "Grip the wheel and drive straight while you slow down," he said aloud to himself, remembering the mantra from high school driver's ed. He stole a glance at the dashboard clock and saw it was just past one-thirty. Normally the drive from Harper's Lake to Cedar Hill took a little over twenty minutes; at this rate he'd be lucky to get there in under an hour.

He saw the flashing of lights above the tree tops from a mile away, and when he rounded the bend a few minutes later the scene before him was utter chaos. A sheriff's car blocked the left lane, the red and blue lights atop it dizzying and blinding. Beyond was an ambulance and a firetruck, and another cruiser blocked the road from the other direction. A small blue pickup lay upside-down at the edge of the woods, its top crushed, its windows curtained by the deployed airbags, the snow around it muddy and obscenely smeared all the way to the pavement. Several men in heavy coveralls stood around the overturned vehicle in the glare of the lights, and Lee realized they were attempting to pry off the driver's door with what he assumed was a "jaws of life" apparatus.

A burly uniformed shadow approached his Escalade. Lee slid the window down and braced himself against the rush of icy wind and snow. "What's going on?"

The shadow tipped his hat back and revealed the round face of a young mustachioed deputy. "Evening, sir. Where you headed?"

"Harper's Lake. Everyone okay?"

"Road that way's a mess," the deputy said, ignoring Lee's question.

"Will I be able to make it through?"

The deputy nodded. "Just take it slow and easy." He chucked a thumb at the Escalade. "Got four-wheel-drive?"

"Yes."

"Make sure you use it."

"Will do."

The deputy motioned him around the cruiser. "Drive safely."

Lee closed the window and eased the Cadillac past the accident scene. He took one last glance at the overturned truck, at the mud caked on the tires and the frantic efforts to cut away the crumpled door, and headed off into the snowy darkness. Another deputy waved him on; Lee caught the man's gaze and nodded. The deputy nodded back, his face tight and grim.

The snow was heavier now, and if not for the slushy tracks in the other lane made by the emergency vehicles, the road would have been impossible to follow. Lee gripped the wheel tighter, as if he could keep the Escalade on the pavement by sheer will. The snow swirled and danced in the glare of the headlights, mesmerizing and dizzying, and he found himself watching the flakes instead of the faint path beyond them.

By the time he reached the hill just outside of Harper's Lake, a cold sweat had beaded on his forehead. Here at least the plows had been through, and as he descended into the town he was surprised at how clear the streets were. To his left the lake was a black void beyond the thick wall of falling snow; to his right the streetlights were blinding in the swirl of white. The storefronts stood quiet and empty, like a vacant set in a cavernous movie studio. The clock on the sign of

Harper's Lake Bank & Trust read 2:17 and twenty-seven degrees. He shivered. He still had to make it out to the turnoff to the cabin, and then down the narrow twisting lane to the house. He took a deep breath and settled into his seat.

The brightness of the town fell behind, and he climbed the hill into the darkness once more. The plows had come only to Saunders' Market, where they had evidently turned around and headed back into Harper's Lake. Lee brought the Escalade to a stop, perched at the top of the snow-covered lane that led down into the blackness toward the cabin. He could park here at the store and walk the rest of the way to the house, he thought. Mr. Saunders wouldn't mind. But the idea of a two-mile trek on foot through blowing snow and bitter wind didn't appeal to him in the least, nor did the very real possibility of falling into a ditch, breaking a bone, and freezing to death before he could be found. He took a deep breath and guided the Escalade down between the skeletal arch of winter branches, as if he were descending into a cave.

Surprisingly, the pavement was easy to discern. The interlocking trees formed a canopy over the road, blocking out the worst of the drifting snow. And while the flakes continued to churn in the headlights, this was nothing like the near-whiteout conditions he'd gone through between Cedar Hill and Harper's Lake. The stand of locust trees emerged from the darkness and beyond them the drive to the house. The walkway lights glowed dimly behind the cabin, outlining the roof against a swirling gray backdrop. He pulled off the paved road and felt the satisfying crunch of gravel beneath the Escalade's wheels. He had made it. He sat in the dark for a moment, listening to the tick of the cooling engine and breathing deeply. He'd been correct – the drive from Cedar Hill had taken a full hour.

He climbed from the Escalade and slogged his way toward the front door. The snow was already ankle-deep and sifting into the tops of his shoes. Thank God he hadn't tried to walk from the highway; his feet would have frozen.

Inside the door he stamped off the snow and wriggled out of his coat and shoes, then stumbled into the living room and switched on a lamp. On the sofa, the kitten looked up where she lay and blinked in the sudden brightness. He reached down and stroked her between the ears and she rose to her feet, stretching and yawning, and leaping down to rub against his legs. "You think I wasn't coming home?" he said. She purred and nuzzled him with the side of her face. He headed for the bedroom, unbuttoning his shirt as he climbed the stairs. "Let's go to bed," he told the cat. "I'm ex-hausted."

But after pulling on a t-shirt and a pair of sweats for warmth and crawling beneath the covers, he found himself unable to turn his mind off. His body still smelled of sex, and images flashed through his mind of Kat taking him into her mouth, of tasting her own fingers. Of her hovering over him while his seed trickled from her lips to his. And then he thought of the pills. All those anti-psychotic drugs lined up in her bathroom like jars of candy. He'd never known her to be unhappy or anxious. Moody, yes. But not inordinately so. What had those years between college and now done to her? Maybe he should pore over those poems in her book again and try to piece it all together.

The years with Mike must have been trying, not to mention the overwhelming betrayal she felt when she discovered he'd been unfaithful. It would be enough to send anyone onto a path of depression. And he wondered whether the medication had expounded her sexual appetite, if what they'd shared tonight had been more than almost two decades of pent-up need. If instead of making love to the Kat he'd once known he had just been fucking a stranger whose libido was only fired up with drugs and alcohol.

But no. She was Kat. She was *still* Kat no matter what the intervening years had done to her. And he knew he still loved her. Had never stopped loving her, even when he struggled to convince himself he loved Jessie. And whatever she was going through now, whatever hell her battered spirit was enduring, he'd stand by her. They'd conquer it together. He'd been too long away from her to let her slip away now, either physically or mentally.

He turned onto his side and felt the kitten slink up beside him and settle in against his chest, purring, her tiny paws kneading the blanket beneath her. After a moment she curled into a ball and the purrs faded away. He closed his eyes and waited for sleep, feeling the kitten's body rise and fall with her breath.

He had almost drifted off, was to the point where dreamlike images were dancing across his vision like the snowflakes he'd driven through earlier, when a tiny noise jolted him awake.

A whisper.

He lay with his eyes wide open, staring into the nothingness, his heart hammering in his chest. Surely he had dreamed it, some auditory hallucination brought on by fatigue. But just as he had convinced himself that what he had heard wasn't real, it came again.

"*Nicky.*"

He sat up, a cry escaping him, knocking the kitten off the bed. She scrambled across the floor and scurried out of the room and down the stairs.

And then he saw her. A young woman. Standing at the foot of the bed. Barely visible in the dim light. No more than a whisper of bluish-gray mist, really. But he could see her clothes – cutoff shorts and a ragged t-shirt – wet and dripping. Her hair clung to her scalp and shoulders like limp seaweed. Her mouth yawned open. "*Nicky.*" Her eyes! He realized with dawning horror that her eyes were gone, replaced with gaping black holes. She reached a shriveled hand out toward him.

He leaped toward the bedside table, grabbing desperately for the lamp, afraid to take his eyes off the girl standing before him. His reaching fingers found the switch and flicked it on, flooding the room with light.

There was nothing there.

IV

Flame

WHEN HE AWOKE the room was filled with gray light so dim it didn't even cast shadows. He lay staring at the beamed ceiling a few moments, wondering whether what he'd seen during the night had been just an illusion or a vivid dream. He knew he'd been tired; it had been a long day, an eventful evening with Kat, and a tortuous drive back to the cabin. He'd had such hallucinations before, back in college when he was sleep deprived during finals. One evening he'd been convinced a young boy was sitting on the roof of the cafeteria; Lee could see him from the dorm window, huddled over and shivering in the December air. He'd been so sure of what he was seeing that he'd telephoned campus security, but as he was on the line with them, the figure atop the cafeteria disappeared, and he never saw it again. That time he'd been going for almost seventy-two hours straight, pumped full of caffeine and No-Doz, and he remembered the jittery feeling of being detached from reality, how his body felt as if he was wearing a rubber suit, how even his teeth felt spongy and foreign in his mouth. But last night he'd felt none of that, only the normal overtiredness of a forty-year-old man still trying to behave as if he were twenty-two.

The kitten leaped onto the bed with a soft meow and rubbed her face against his scruffy cheek. "Hey there," he said, stroking her back. She arched to meet his hand, purring contentedly. "Why don't you make yourself useful and go put on some coffee?"

He sat up in the bed, his head fuzzy and unfocused, and looked toward the window. Snow continued to fall, large flakes that came down quickly like rain. Had it been like that all night?

He pulled himself out of the warmth of the bed and shivered as he stared out at the whitish-gray world beyond the glass. The lake was invisible through the snowfall; in fact, he couldn't make out much past the edge of the deck, only the vague hint of the tree line at the edge of the yard. He was glad he'd come on home last night. As much as he'd enjoyed the evening with Kat, being snowed in with her was not something he wanted to experience just yet. He was still married, after all, and deep down some Puritanical morals that had hidden themselves during the previous evening's activities still frowned upon spending the entire night with another woman. Especially one he was sure Jessie would freak out over.

Downstairs he checked the thermostat. Still seventy-two. And though he'd traded his light sleep attire for a sweatshirt and baggy jeans, he was still shivering. He inched the indicator to seventy-three, thought a moment, then moved it on to seventy-four. The furnace sprang to life, and he immediately felt warmer just hearing the thrum of the unit.

His cellphone rang, and he immediately felt a sting of panic. He'd completely forgotten the conference call with Bill. He'd planned to come up with something to stall him some more, even if it was just some bullshit story. But now he'd fucked around and hadn't even thought of writing since Bill's email on Sunday.

He looked at the screen and was immediately relieved to see it was the home phone in Springfield. "Hey," he said.

"Hi, Dad!" came Corey's excited voice. "Did you see the snow?"

Lee grinned; the boy's enthusiasm was contagious. "I sure did!"

"We didn't go to school today!"

"Nice!"

"Nana says we may be out the rest of the week!"

"Really?"

"That's what Nana says. But I hope I can still come down to stay with you this weekend."

Lee glanced at the patio doors. There was nothing beyond the glass but a swirling world of white. "Well, we'll see," he said. "Depends on what the weather does."

"Okay."

"Is your mom there? Can I talk to her?"

"Nope. She's at work. She stayed overnight at the TV station. Nana's been here since yesterday. We got to stay up late last night and watch movies. Nana made popcorn. On the stove, not in the microwave. It was so good! She said – "

"Can I talk to her? To Nana?"

"Sure."

Lee heard the receiver drop and Corey calling for Jessie's mom. While he waited he fixed the coffee, careful to dig around through the container to make sure no nasty surprises had manifested themselves since yesterday. He had no idea what he would do if that happened again. Coffee was essential, and if he couldn't have it the situation would be dire.

The line on the other end rustled, and a pleasant female voice said, "Hi, Lee."

"Hey, Barbara. How're things going up there?"

"Well, you can just imagine. I've got a seven-year-old bouncing off the walls to get out and play in the blizzard and a twelve-year-old pissed off at the world because the internet's down here."

Lee couldn't help but laugh. He'd never before heard Jessie's mother use the term "pissed off." He pulled a mug from the cabinet. "The internet's down?"

"Yep. Has been since last night."

"Did you check the modem? Lizbeth knows how to do that."

"It's out all over town," Barbara said. "Some major connection down due to the storm. They have no idea when it will get fixed."

"Wow," Lee said, looking again at the billowing gusts of snow outside the patio doors, "I had no idea it was that bad."

"We measured this morning on your back patio. Thirteen inches and still coming down to beat the band. Snowplows can't keep up. They say we could have over two feet before all's said and done."

"Did Jessie have any trouble making it in to work?"

"She went in yesterday afternoon," Barbara said.

"Packed a bag for several days. Said she would stay at the station until all this was over."

"Probably a good idea. You have everything you need?"

"We're fine."

"There's an emergency credit card in the top left drawer of the desk in my office if you have to get anything."

"We'll be all right," Barbara said. "And I don't know how we'd get out to get anything anyway. I think we're going to be pretty well stuck for the rest of the week. How is it down at the lake?"

"Pretty bad from what I can see," Lee told her. "But I can't see a lot. Everything's white. I can't even see the water from the house."

"Well, you take care of yourself down there."

"I'll be okay. Tell the kids they can call me anytime."

He hung up and poured a mug of coffee, then seated himself at the dining room table and booted up his laptop. The wind howled around the corner of the house battering the glass doors with snow and ice. The kitten crept toward the sliding doors and settled in to watch the mess outside, occasionally pouncing on the glass at a particularly large snowflake.

He was relieved to see the internet was still working – down here at Harper's Lake anyway. He browsed to the site for Jessie's station and glanced over the headlines. Barbara hadn't been kidding. Blizzard warning. The state had banned all unnecessary travel for the next twenty-four hours. And the weather map showed nothing but a stalled mass of white over the whole region. As ugly as it was now, it was just going to get uglier. Well, he'd wanted some isolation and quiet; looked like now he was going to get plenty of it.

He leaned back in the chair and took a sip of his coffee. Jessie smiled at him from the banner graphic at the top of the webpage. In the picture she wore a red dress with a modest neckline. Her arms were crossed and she was smiling open-mouthed, her blond hair cascading across her shoulders. She was flanked on either side by two chiseled hunks in suits whom Lee recognized as the other morning anchor and the weather man. Guiltily, he found himself wondering whether Jessie had slept with either of them. He couldn't imagine she had, but after last night he was searching for anything to justify his evening with Kat. He looked at Jessie's photo, and chided himself as he realized he couldn't even meet her gaze in the picture.

He checked the time and realized he still had an hour before Bill's call. An hour. Just sixty minutes to come up with something to put him off for a while. Well, that wasn't going to happen. It was time face it: he was dried up. He had nothing left. He'd always envied those writers who could churn out words like some sort of factory, but he was not one of them. Never had been. At conventions he'd sat in bars with writers who claimed five or six thousand words a day, and sometimes the odd bird who boasted upwards of ten thousand, but he'd never understood how anyone could think that fast. They seemed to be mindless machines, pecking away at keyboards with nary a thought as to what they were committing to paper. With the exception of the first Max Plexico book, he'd always struggled for the words to come. Always. As if when he sat down in front of the blank screen his mind was suddenly befuddled and thick. Most days he labored to eke out a few hundred words. Quick writing had never been his strength, although his first drafts usually required little editing; in fact, the last few Max Plexico books had not been edited at all, save for a typo check. But in any event, no one could edit something that wasn't being written. And it didn't look like either would happen.

His phone buzzed again, and again he felt a stab of panic. But it was Harvey. Checking up on him, no doubt. "Hey there."

"Lee, it's Harvey. Just checking up on ya."

Bingo. "Yeah, Harvey. Everything's all right."

"You all set for the storm? Looks like it's gonna last a few days."

"Yep, I'm good. Plenty of food, plenty of firewood in case the power goes out. How about you?"

"I'll be all right. This ain't my first rodeo, you know."

"I'm sure." He sipped his coffee. "Talked to my mother-in-law. She says we could get two feet."

"That's what I heard, too. Sometimes we get a little more down here on the lake, though. Something about how the wind comes off the water."

"Yeah, it's coming down so thick I can't even *see* the water."

"How's the little one?" Harvey asked, and Lee realized he was asking about the kitten.

"Fine. She's watching the snow."

"Got a name for her yet?"

"No. Right now she's just 'Cat.'" He smiled to himself, thinking of the irony. He looked at her, staring intently at the falling flakes. "I don't know. . . maybe Grace. Or Gracie." The name echoed through his brain, and he wondered where he'd heard it recently.

"Gracie's cute," Harvey said.

"Yeah. I like that. Gracie." The kitten turned and stared at him. "I think she likes it, too."

"Hey, I gotta go," Harvey said. "You got my number, you call if you need anything."

"Same here," Lee said. "I'll save a cup of coffee for you for the next time you come by."

"You do that."

He set the phone down and stared at the snow through the patio doors. If he concentrated, he could almost see shapes appearing in the swirling gray – faces, bodies, animals. His mind was playing with him, he knew. An effect known as *pareidolia*, and what the investigators on those ghost hunting shows called "matrixing." His brain merely trying to make sense out of the chaos of shadow and light. It was mesmerizing, hypnotizing. The dark gray mass of the trees beyond also seemed to be moving, inching closer like rainclouds. The shape took on the semblance of a person moving closer, floating toward the deck.

The body hit the door with a thump that rattled the walls, knocking a framed print to the floor with a shatter of glass. The kitten scurried off into the recesses of the cabin. Lee could only sit and stare.

A man. Or what had once been a man. Waterlogged and rotten, the skin gray and sloughing away, the face swollen and green, the dark hair patchy and muddy. The eyes, white and marbled, stared out at him through blackened slits. It raised a fist, a fist that was covered in slime and muck, and banged it against the glass door.

Lee was on his feet at once, his heart pounding explosively in his chest, his arms and legs tingling with fright. "Who are you? What do you want?"

The man pounded on the door again, leaving a black, putrid smear across the glass. The mouth opened like a gaping wound, and brown water and gritty silt poured out.

Lee realized the figure was wearing a shredded tank top – *a wife-beater*, his mind screamed insanely – and the rags of what had once been red swim trunks. It was barefoot.

Lee backed away, stumbling into the dining chair. It fell over with a clatter. He couldn't take his eyes from the creature at the door. And with dawning horror, he realized what – *who* – he was looking at. "Oh my god. *Nicky*?"

The cell phone rang, shrill and sudden. Lee glanced at it, and some remaining bit of sanity in his brain noted that it was Bill calling. He looked back at the patio doors.

The figure was gone.

Lee stood looking at the empty door, at the swirling snow beyond, wondering what, if anything, he'd actually seen.

The phone continued to ring. Blindly, he grabbed for it and stabbed at the screen to answer it. "Hello."

"Lee? Is that you?"

"Yes, it's me."

"You don't sound like yourself."

Lee kept his gaze glued to the patio door. "Must be the connection."

Bill chuckled on the other end. "Could be. Looks like you folks are getting hammered down there."

"Yeah." Lee realized a light cold sweat glazed his forehead. He wiped at it absently. "Hammered."

Bill cleared his throat. "Well, I won't beat around the bush. You know why I'm calling."

"Yeah."

"You given any thought to my email?"

Lee tore his gaze away from the patio doors and looked at his laptop screen. He fumbled to open his mailbox and found Bill's message from Saturday.

"Lee, you there?"

"I'm here." He scrolled through the lines of text, seeing them but unable to read them. Letters on the screen. That's all they were. A jumbled mass of letters. No sense. Nothing was making sense.

"Lee – "

"Jessie and I are separated, Bill."

Bill was silent for a moment. "I'm sorry to hear that."

"I'm at the lake cabin. Alone. I'm trying to sort out my life. I'm trying to figure things out." As soon as the words slipped out of his lips, he realized they were the same ones Kat had spoken the night before, and a sense of deep sadness settled over him, drowning out the terror he had felt just moments before. "I need some time, Bill."

Bill sighed heavily. "Lee, you've had eighteen months."

"I know."

"As I said in my email, if Circle doesn't have something – "

Lee slammed a palm against the dining table. "God*dammit*, Bill! Are you not listening to a fucking thing I'm telling you? My life is falling apart. My marriage is over. I can't think, let alone write. I have no idea what I'm fucking doing anymore."

"It's nothing personal, Lee. It's just. . . business."

"Well, fuck it," Lee said, spittle flying from his mouth. "Fuck you, and fuck Circle, and fuck the contract."

"Lee, you know breaching the contract will mean you'll have to pay back the advance."

Lee took a deep breath and closed his eyes. "Right now I don't give a good goddamn. I'll send them a check as soon as I get back home." He leaned back in his chair and was surprised to feel tears coursing down his cheeks. "I'm tired, Bill. I'm just. . . tired."

"Lee, are you okay? Are you seeing someone, a counselor or something?"

"No." He wiped away the tears with the back of his hand and massaged his temples where a dull ache had started. "I just need some rest. I just need to not think for a while."

"Do you think you should go back home? Should you call Jessie?"

"Absolutely not. And for god's sake, don't you call her either."

"I wouldn't do that, Lee."

"I couldn't get home right now even if I wanted to. I'm stuck out here until this storm is over. Could be days."

"So," Bill said, "what do I tell Tom Feeney at Circle? Are you sure you want out of this contract? You know what it will mean."

Lee took a deep breath. "Tell Tom Feeney to roll up that contract and shove it up his ass."

Bill sighed. "All right. But Lee, you know if you do this I'll have to end my association with you."

"I know," Lee said, but in his mind he thought, *Liar*.

"It's going to be very difficult for you to find another agent, and *damn* difficult to find another publisher willing to work with you."

"I don't care at this point," Lee said. "I just don't want to do this anymore. I don't think I even want to write anymore." Saying the words, speaking aloud what he had felt inside him for so long came with a wave of relief.

"I don't think you mean that," Bill said.

"I do mean it," Lee told him. "I'm burned out, Bill. I'm burned out, dried up, and completely exhausted. At some point I may get back to it, but if I do it will be on my terms, not out of obligation to some fucking contract. I'm done, Bill. I'm done."

"Okay," Bill said softly. "If that's what you really want."

"It is."

"We'll get some papers drawn up and I'll send them out to you. Termination of Agency Relationship and all that."

"Okay."

Bill sat quietly, as if waiting for Lee to change his mind. "I've enjoyed working with you, Lee. I wish you the best of luck. Professionally and personally."

"Thanks," Lee said, and before Bill could say anything else, Lee disconnected the call.

He sat staring out at the falling snow, at where the figure – Nicky – had stood at the doorway. There were no footprints in the snow that had drifted across the deck. But as Lee looked closer, he saw something that made his heart stop.

Where Nicky had pounded on the glass, a dark smear of lake sludge remained.

* * *

By noon the drifts on the deck were a third of the way up the patio doors. The day remained dark and gray, and still the snow fell. Lee no longer tried to view the lake, as there was nothing beyond the faint tree line but a whitish-gray mass. And after what he'd seen that morning, he avoided looking out the windows at all. Out front, the Escalade was buried to the bumper. There would be no getting out any time soon, even if the snow stopped now, which the forecast claimed it would not.

He and the cat curled up together on the couch. He had ditched Poe for an old Ira Levin paperback, *The Boys from Brazil*, and while he read, Gracie lay next to him and purred in her sleep. Gradually, the the words began to run together, and he finally set the book down and succumbed to a nap.

He awoke a little after two-thirty. The house was darker, and the snow continued to fall. He glanced at his phone and saw he'd had a message from Kat a little after one. *Hey, what's up? Had fun last night.*

He tapped out, *Hey there, me too*, and pressed send.

After a moment, the phone buzzed with a response. *Oh hey. Thought you were ignoring me.*

He smiled. As if anyone could ignore Kat. *Napping lol.*

Did I wear you out?

Something stirred within him, sending an electric twinge to his cock. *Uh huh.*

She replied with a smiley-face emoji.

He was typing out a response when the phone rang with her incoming call. "I was just texting you back," he said.

"It's easier to talk," she said, and her voice was like

velvet.

He felt a grin spreading across his face. "Well, hello there."

"Hi."

He rolled over onto his side, staring at the dying light through the curtains. "Still snowing," he said.

"Yes, and I worried about you all night. I should have texted you to make sure you made it home."

"I should have let you know I got here okay," he said. "It was a wild ride."

"It got cold here after you left. And lonely."

"Uh huh. It was here, too." His mind flashed to the image of the girl standing at the foot of his bed in the night, and he pushed it away. "We'll have to get together again soon."

"I hope I didn't come off as too aggressive," Kat said. "Or desperate, which is even worse."

"You weren't either," Lee told her. "And besides, I was too horny to care."

She laughed, but her voice sounded tired and sad. "You haven't changed much over the years. You were always up for a good fuck."

He chuckled, but something deep within him cringed. The way she'd said it. As if their night together had just been *fucking*, not *making love*. And, he supposed, in a way it had been. "Well, I hope you don't think that's all it was."

"I don't."

They fell into an awkward silence, and finally he said, "They say we might get two feet of snow."

"That's what I heard," she said. "The college has already called off classes for tomorrow."

"Ah," Lee said, "so you get a couple of days off."

"Well," she said, "A couple of days to sit and brood. At least you're being productive."

"I am?"

"Yeah, writing. I'm just sitting here drinking tea and pretending to read and listening to Adele."

Lee grunted. She didn't know how pathetically dried up he'd become. "Yeah," he said softly.

"Getting much done?"

"I am," he lied, and wondered why he was doing so.

"So. . . what are you working on? A new novel? A new Max Plexico? You didn't say much about it."

"A novel," he said. He glanced back at the patio doors. At the lake sludge smear on the glass and the swirling storm beyond. "A horror novel."

"Really? Horror? That's quite a departure for you, isn't it?"

"Hitting pretty close to home these days," he said.

"Really? How so?"

Lee snuggled against the kitten and she woke with a purr and stretched her legs. "Well, let's just say being out here alone has definitely played on my imagination."

"Yeah, I'm not sure I could handle all that quiet. And the isolation. How are you coping with that?"

Lee glanced back at the patio doors, at the nothingness beyond the glass. "Okay, I guess. Still have the internet. And the phone. So it's not like I'm completely cut off."

"Well, that's something." She moaned a bit, and Lee imagined her lying among the twisted sheets on her bed that still smelled of their lovemaking, stretching. She would be wearing silky panties and an old t-shirt – her favorite sleep attire. But she would have brushed her hair and her teeth, even if she was feeling particularly lazy.

When he remembered details like that, details from their former stint as lovers, he felt a hollow pang in his chest. It was a hurt he didn't feel when he thought of Jessie, and that lack of hurt produced a completely different emotion: Guilt. How could he feel so emotionless toward a woman he had spent so many years with? With whom he'd fathered two children? A woman with whom he'd built a life and a home? It was simple, really. He felt nothing for her now because she had shown him nothing in all that time together. Jessie had always been about Jessie. Everything had been for how she looked to outsiders – the house, the career. Even the way she dressed Corey and Lizbeth. She'd wanted everyone to know the Houstons were successful. Prosperous. Wealthy. While behind the walls of their cookie-cutter mansion she was distant and cold, and the fire of their love had died out to lifeless ashes long ago. It made him sick. He wondered why and how he'd remained faithful all that time. They'd abandoned lovemaking altogether the last year or so, and Lee had been left to secretive solitary pleasures when he could chance them. Not that he hadn't had chances, especially when he'd gone on book tours and made appearances at conventions. But that sense of morality – of duty – had always been at the back of his mind policing his actions, even when he wasn't consciously aware of it.

"Oh, shit," Kat said suddenly.

"What is it?"

"The power just went out." He listened as she shuffled through her apartment. "I can't tell if it's just my building or... Wait. No, it's the whole street."

"Well that sucks. Do you still have heat?"

"Oh, yeah. This old building still has radiators and a gas-fired boiler. I'm not gonna freeze."

"That's good."

"What about you? If your power goes out will you be able to stay warm down there?"

"I've got a fireplace and enough wood to last the next two months. I'll be fine." He scratched the kitten idly behind her ears. "Wish you were here, though. It would be a lot cozier."

"If I was there, you wouldn't get any writing done," she said.

He grunted. "Yeah."

"Or anything else."

He laughed. "Probably."

"I'll let you go. Call me later, okay?"

"Will do."

He disconnected the call and tossed the phone to the other end of the sofa. Gracie watched it fly over her head, then pounced after it. He chuckled and grabbed for her, tickling her belly and minding the needle-like sharpness of her tiny claws. She rolled over onto her side and looked at him, blinking. "So," he said, "come here often?"

He gave her one last pat and dragged himself off the sofa, stretching and staring at the white outside. The dark smudge on the glass of the patio door bothered him. Had he imagined the whole thing? Had the smudge been on the door all this time without him noticing it? And why had he just assumed the figure he saw was Nicky? He moved closer to the door. No footprints or tracks of any kind marked the snow, yet the dirt was black against the stark background like a giant comma. He took a step backward and felt a sharp pain in his foot. "Fuck!"

He looked down to see a shard of glass embedded in his heel. The white sock on his foot was already blooming red with blood. "God*dammit!*" He must have missed a piece when he'd cleaned up the shattered picture.

The picture Nicky knocked off the wall with his urgent pounding.

He reached down and gingerly pulled out the sliver, wincing against the sharp stab of pain as he did so. He managed to limp upstairs to the bathroom and pull off the blood-soaked sock, then grabbed a wash cloth, doused it with cold water and pressed it against the wound. It took several minutes of compressing before the bleeding stopped and he was able to examine the gash. Though it was no longer oozing blood, the laceration was deep. Maneuvering the skin gave him a queasy feeling in the middle of his gut. He would need stitches. And with the storm outside, there was no way he could get to a doctor. He would have to do it himself.

He had researched self-suturing for the second-to-last Max Plexico book for a scene in which Max was stranded in the Australian Outback, and he was fairly certain that he remembered the steps involved. But writing about it and doing it were two separate matters. At this point, though, he had no choice. An open wound of this sort could lead to infection and gangrene and, in possibly the worst-case scenario, amputation.

In the bedroom he fumbled through the top drawer of the bureau until he found Jessie's little sewing kit –

one she'd brought to darn holes and re-attach stray buttons – and carried it back to the bathroom sink. This would require some doing. There was at least a silver gadget to thread the tiny needle – perfect for forty-year-old eyes and thick fingers.

He pulled the bottle of rubbing alcohol from beneath the sink and took a seat on the closed toilet. Dangling his foot over the tub, he uncapped the bottle and poured its contents liberally over his injured heel.

The pain seared like a hot poker. "Son of a *bitch!*" All he could do for a moment was ball up and wait for the burning agony to subside. And when at last the pain faded, he realized he'd been holding his breath since the alcohol touched him. "Fuck. Oh, fuck."

With quaking fingers he managed to douse the needle and the black thread he'd worked through it with more alcohol. He hunched over his throbbing foot, the tip of the needle poised just above the skin, summoning the courage to begin. This was going to hurt.

He took a deep breath. Pierced the needle through the flesh. He watched, fascinated, as it crossed beneath the tear in his skin and came out the other side. The pain had become like some far away part of him, disassociated with the act of sewing up the wound. He crossed the stitch across the cut, feeling the skin pull with the pressure, then pricked the needle through the flesh again, repeated the motion, drawing the edges of the cut together. By the fifth stitch he no longer felt any pain. The wound was numb, and sewing the skin of his heel felt like trussing a chicken. He finished the job, then looked at his work, wondering if he should pour more alcohol over the jagged sutures.

The nausea hit him suddenly, and he doubled over

and retched into the tub. The stench of his vomit along with the sight of his injury forced his stomach to heave again, and he spewed forth a hot stream of sour tasting bile. He laid his cheek against the edge of the tub and closed his eyes, forcing the the spinning sickness to dissipate. He sat hunched like that for some time, until a stiffness in his lower back forced him to stand.

Lee bandaged his wound as best he could. The cut was on the bottom of his heel, so walking would be awkward the next few days. He hobbled down the stairs to the living room and poured a finger of bourbon, then settled back on the sofa, resting his foot on a pillow atop the coffee table.

He reached for the Ira Levin book and his reading glasses, grunting as he doubled over his growing gut, and lay back against the cushions. He opened the book to the marked page, but after one paragraph, he closed his eyes and placed the book face-down on his chest. Reading required too much brain power, which he didn't seem to have.

Gracie hopped onto the couch and crept onto his stomach and stood there, purring, until Lee moved the paperback, giving her room to settle down on his chest. She kneaded his shirt, her purrs almost deafening, then eased down on top of him. He stroked her back, and she arched to meet his fingertips, then quickly hunkered back down, her paws continuing to mechanically knead him, her eyes half-closed and drowsy.

When exactly he fell asleep again he didn't know. But he knew he was sleeping because he was back in the country, back at his grandparents' farm in west Tennessee. It was summer, and the air was thick and warm, and the deep colors of dusk had settled over the countryside. He was heading for the old orchard, winding down an abandoned weed-choked lane, the field grass sharp and rough beneath his bare feet. He looked down and was surprised to find he was naked except for the bandage around his foot. Beneath his flabby, loose stomach his shriveled penis lolled obscenely. He tried to cover himself, but he couldn't move his hands. Still he walked on, aware of the vague throb of his heel.

Once when he was a boy, the dozen or so trees here produced large, juicy fruit. Granddaddy would take him in the rattling, decrepit pickup truck down the dirt road at dusk. The sun would be down but there would be just enough light to see. The apples had been big then, big and green and tart. While Granddaddy sat perched with a cigarette on the folded-down tailgate of the truck, Lee would fill a bushel basket with as many apples as he could carry. And as Lee gathered apples, Grandmama would gather cherries from the single cherry tree at the back of the orchard, reaching up as high as she could to pick them and drop them into a little saucepan she carried. Each year she had a devil of a time keeping the birds from them, and she would tie tin pie plates up in the branches so the wind would bang them together and scare the birds off. The birds got used to the noise after a while, but somehow Grandmama always managed to save enough to can and make pies. After they had gathered all their fruit, they would make their way back to the house under the early evening sky with Lee riding in the truck bed eating a fresh apple from the bushel basket.

But now he was standing under a lacy tunnel of bare branches, wild and unruly, and brown, rotten apples dotted the neglected grounds. The stump of the cherry tree, cut down when it became fragile and dangerous after Grandmama died, gleaned in the dying light. He could see Granddaddy's old rusted Chevrolet pickup, the same faded blue he remembered, and Granddaddy was sitting in his accustomed place on the tailgate, the fire of his cigarette glowing a brilliant orange. Grandmama was also there, staring up at the tops of the trees. In her hands were two tin pie plates, and she was beating them together relentlessly. She turned and caught sight of Lee, and her dark eyes narrowed behind her cat's eye glasses. "Scat your ass!" she hollered. "You done went and cut down my cherry tree! Now all them birds is here in my apple trees. You git yourself back to the house!"

Lee strained but he could hear no birds in the trees. Only the steady, drowsy drone of crickets and the occasional ratcheting of a cicada. He tried to tell her this but his throat was locked up tight. He headed back up the road in the dim light. Neither of them had noticed he was naked.

This was a dream, right? Everything was in such clarity – the buzz of insects, the jagged gravel beneath his bare feet that seemed to pierce through the bandage on his heel, the heady smell of fresh-cut timothy, the pinpoints of the first stars in the deep blue twilit sky. Even the salty taste of the stream of sweat trickling down his upper lip. If this was a dream it was damned vivid.

As he lumbered down the road, he passed a grove of fir trees. On the back side was a large swimming pool surrounded by a high brick wall. He opened the iron gate with a squeak and stepped into the area. The concrete deck was cracked and blackened with time. Weeds pushed through to the surface, some nearly knee-high. But the lights in the spotless pool were aglow beneath the warm blue water, changing shape as waves rippled the surface. He turned and saw Jessie standing high on a diving board, its surface mottled with green mold. She was dressed in a smart navy-blue suit – a suit she sometimes wore on television. "You bum," she called down to him. "You're nothing but a good-for-nothing lazy asshole." She cast her narrow cold eyes down to the water. "I'm glad you left me, you know. You can't expect me to work and support you while you lie around and do nothing but go off to sleep with other women." She looked back at him. "Although I can't imagine what kind of whore would want to sleep with the likes of *you*." She took her position and dove in gracefully, high-heeled shoes and all. He rushed to the edge of the pool to look for her, but she was gone. The bottom of the pool was smooth and empty.

He stepped out of the pool area, and as the iron gate clanged shut behind him, he turned to see that the lights had gone out. In the dim light of the early evening he could just make out the pit of the swimming pool. An empty, cracked concrete pit full of dirt and rotting stray tree branches and murky, putrid water. The diving board dangled oddly, held precariously by a single screw.

He trudged up the gravel lane, mindful of his throbbing heel, heading for a house nearby. It was Granddaddy and Grandmama's place, that old ramshackle, white-clapboard farmhouse with the concrete porch and the creaky screen door. He could see lamps burning inside. He made his way across the yard, the grass wet with dew, through the door and into the kitchen. There was no one there. He went on through the house, the eerie silence prickling the back of his neck like the light touch of a feather. He moved up the narrow stairs, each step creaking beneath his weight.

He finally found himself in Grandmama and Granddaddy's dark, sparse bedroom. Someone lay beneath the covers of the bed. The sprawled limbs were still, but Lee could faintly see the stomach rising and falling with breath. Gathering his courage, he grasped the edge of the sheet and whipped it back.

It was Kat. She giggled and sat up. She was also naked, and her full breasts peeked above the top of the cover. Her nipples were stiff and rigid. "I fixed everything," she told him, smiling behind her hand. "Look out the window. I fixed it all for you." Lee hesitated. "Go on," she said.

He stepped across the room and peered through a part in the curtains to see a cherry tree, its boughs straining with the burden of ripe fruit. In the branches, Lizbeth and Corey sat together, gathering handfuls of cherries and stuffing them into their mouths, eating pits and all, the juice running down their chins like bloody drool. They turned to look at him, and their eyes glowed white with the light of the sun. Lee shivered.

And then he could feel Kat's arms around his waist. Her hand slithered down, brushing across his pubic hair to grasp his stiffening penis. Her fingers were like ice, but he found himself growing harder with her touch. He turned to her and she held him tight, running her fingers over the small of his back. Her nipples stabbed his chest, rubbing against him as she moved, and his erection pressed against her stomach.

They fell together on the bed and he entered her smoothly and easily. They were a bundle of writhing, sweating, moaning flesh, moving toward a high, fever-pitched climax when everything would vanish.

* * *

He awoke with a start, his face hot and sweating, his erection straining against his jeans. The room was nearly pitch-black. Gracie was gone. He fumbled with his fly and freed himself, then masturbated frantically to an almost pleasureless orgasm.

He lay panting, his heart racing and his fingers shaking as he continued to grasp his shrinking erection. He dragged himself off the sofa and shuffled upstairs to clean himself off. Going up was much more difficult on his wounded heel than coming down had been, and he worried that the pressure of the steps would tear open the cut. But the sutures he'd given himself held, and though walking was painful he was relieved to see no tell-tale spots of blood seeping through his bandage.

There was no way he could shower. Not with the dressing over his wound. He filled the sink with hot water and stripped off his clothing, then bathed from the basin as best he could. By the time he was finished, he was shivering in the cold air. He dressed quickly in the bedroom and looked at the mound of dirty clothing piled in the corner. He needed to do laundry. Already. And he'd only been here four days. Lugging the clothing downstairs to the washing machine would be a problem now with his heel. He blew out a breath. He would deal with it tomorrow, and hopefully his foot would be better.

In the living room he checked the thermostat. Still at seventy-four. He shivered. Why was it so fucking cold in here?

Outside the patio doors, the light was a soft purple. The snow continued to fall and he could see nothing but a gray void beyond the deck railing, not even the trees at the edge of the yard. The drifts against the glass were now up to his waist; he'd carried in several armloads of firewood and stocked the rack next to the fireplace, but he wondered if he needed more how he would dig through to the lean-to to get any.

His stomach rumbled, and he realized he hadn't had anything to eat since his dinner last night with Kat. He'd only had coffee and bourbon, and very little of that. He flipped on the light in the kitchen – blinking against the sudden brightness – and dug through the freezer until he found something that looked remotely appetizing. Macaroni and cheese. He popped it in the microwave and waited for it to heat.

He still hadn't seen Gracie, and he wondered where she'd wandered off to. He pulled out a tin of cat food and dumped its contents onto a small plate, then set it down beside her water bowl. "Gracie? Dinner!" The microwave beeped and shut itself off, and Lee stood still listening for the kitten to come scrambling for her food.

Nothing. Silence.

"Gracie? Kitty kitty?"

Where had the stupid thing gone off to? Was she in her litter box? He moved into the laundry room and flipped on the light.

He stared at the smears of blood across the white linoleum for almost a full minute before he comprehended what he was seeing. Bright red, leading to a dark corner on the other side of the dryer. "Gracie? Are you all right?"

He stepped over the blood and moved toward the dryer, a wave of horror washing over him.

Gracie lay on her side, her eyes open and glazed, one front paw stretched out as if reaching for him, her colorless tongue lolling from her mouth. Something had ripped into her, chewing into her stomach and leaving the flesh ragged and torn. The blood had come from her belly and had pooled beneath her; it had already dried some in her matted fur. Lee realized she must have been dead for a couple of hours, probably since right after he'd drifted off to sleep on the couch.

He sat back, staring at her, his body numb. What had done this? What could have fought with the kitten and shredded her belly without waking him? It must have been quick, and he hoped for her sake that she hadn't suffered.

He whirled around, checking to see if anything else was in the laundry room with him, hiding in a dark corner or behind the appliances. Nothing. Whatever had done this to Gracie was gone. At least from this room.

He looked back at the kitten with a mixture of sadness, revulsion, and shock. He wasn't surprised to feel tears coursing down his cheeks.

The gnawing started above his head, loud and grating. He looked to the ceiling, half expecting to see flakes of plaster drifting down like the snow outside. Nothing. Just the sound of that incessant gnawing. It grew louder, now moving through the walls on either side, to the very floor beneath him. He could feel the vibration in his buttocks where he sat. Louder and louder. Deafening. He covered his ears. The sound now seemed to be in his head. Between his ears. Behind his eyes.

"STOP IT!"

And suddenly the gnawing did stop. He sat motionless for a moment, straining to hear. . . he didn't know what. The skittering of animal feet inside the walls? The squeaking of a thousand mice? The lumbering of a fat raccoon above him in the ceiling? But there was nothing but the rush of the wind whipping around the edge of the house.

He grabbed an old towel from the cabinet above the washer and gathered Gracie's little body in it and wiped up the blood. The floor would need a good scrubbing. He grabbed a plastic trash bag from the kitchen and carefully placed her inside it, then tied it off and stood looking at it. What was he going to do with her? He certainly couldn't bury her now, not with two feet of snow outside. And he couldn't very well just place her out on the back deck; some ravenous wild animal might drag her off, and he couldn't stomach the idea of that.

He pulled out another garbage bag and placed the one holding Gracie inside it, rolled both of them up tightly, then gently laid her in the freezer. There was really nothing else he could do with her. Not right now.

He mopped up the blood in the laundry room, gagging at the pungent odor of the bleach water, then scrubbed his hands nearly raw as he tried to wash away the smell. He'd always been sensitive to the scent of bleach, even going so far as to shun swimming pools for the odor of chlorine.

Which made him think of the dream again. Jessie on the high dive.

I'm glad you left me, you know.

He wondered if that were really true. And he figured it probably was. His and Jessie's relationship had died out years ago. The time they'd spent together since had merely been one of convenience and laziness – an unwillingness on either of their parts to actually make a move to end it. If this separation turned out to be permanent, he wasn't worried about her. She was a strong woman. Ambitious. Ruthless. She would be fine. It was the kids he worried about most. Lizbeth was already showing the independent, strong-willed streak so prevalent in Jessie, and while he had no doubt she would grow up to be her own woman, he wondered whether Jessie would be able to handle her alone once she reached her rebellious teen years. Corey on the other hand was thoughtful and introverted; hopefully Jessie could ingrain some of her gregarious nature in him, otherwise Lee feared the world would eat him alive. The universe wasn't kind to sensitive souls.

He pulled the mac and cheese from the microwave and stood at the kitchen counter, shoveling it into his mouth mechanically. It had cooled, and now the cheese sauce was tasteless and grainy. He ate it anyway; he needed food. The heavy bleach smell still hovered in the air, and he knew if it didn't dissipate soon he would become nauseated.

His phone chimed with an incoming message. He hoped it was Jessie. Why, he didn't know, except that he could think of no one else he'd want to hear from. He reached for his phone and glanced at the screen.

Hi Lee.

A jolt bolted through him. It was the same number from the other night, the crazy girl asking for Nicky.

But this time she was calling Lee by name. Had he told her his name? He couldn't remember. He held the phone, contemplating on whether to answer her or just block the number again.

It chimed with another incoming message: *I'm still cold. Is it cold where you are?*

Fuck this. He wasn't doing this again. He blocked the number and tossed the phone to the counter with a clatter.

Immediately the phone buzzed to life. Another message. *Hi Lee.*

He looked at it. A different number. Someone was messing with him. He blocked that number as well, but before he could set the phone down it vibrated again in his hand.

Hi Lee.

He blocked the number, then waited, phone in hand. He did not have to wait long.

Hi Lee.

For a moment he thought of simply turning the phone off. But what if Jessie or her mother or – God forbid – one of the kids tried to reach him? This was obviously someone using a caller ID spoofing app, maybe even a computer. Maybe if he didn't respond they'd just get bored and leave him alone.

Hi Lee.

He shoved another spoonful of macaroni and cheese into his mouth and chewed, staring at the phone as it chimed with another incoming message.

Why are you ignoring me?

He shook his head and reached into the fridge for a drink. Maybe he should lay off the booze and caffeine and go for something healthier. He grabbed a bottle of water and uncapped it just as the phone vibrated again on the counter. He grunted and glanced at the screen.

He froze. His fingers tingled with sudden terror.

Enjoying your mac n cheese?

He set the plastic container and the spoon down on the counter. The food was acid in his gullet. He glanced about the kitchen and beyond, focusing on the shadows in the corners of the living room. "Is somebody here?" he said, aware of the sudden quiver in his voice.

The phone buzzed. *Not that you can see.*

The feeling of horror came over him in waves. He could feel it welling up in his eyes – tears of terror. "Where are you?"

Chime. *You'll never find us.*

He stared at the word "us." There was more than one of them. He thought of the night he'd first received the texts, then the call. When he thought he'd seen someone – *something* – on the deck in the falling darkness. Had they been watching him all this time? Had they been waiting for him when he first got to the cabin? Hiding out somewhere within the house? But he'd checked every room in the cabin, plus the attic when he'd set out the poison. He'd seen no evidence of anyone else's presence. But somehow they were watching him.

Cameras. They must have cameras hidden throughout the house. Maybe running off wi-fi or Bluetooth or something. Terror was beginning to melt into anger. Stalkers. Just like Cameron Fields. What if Cameron were back, just as he'd feared? Or what if it turned out to be worse?

"You like spying on me? Playing peeping tom? Is that how you get your rocks off? Come out! Show yourselves!"

He stood like a stone, listening. Nothing. Not the slightest creak of a floorboard or squeak of a distant hinge.

The phone buzzed with a new message: *You've already seen us.*

His mind swam. The figure at the foot of the bed. The decaying man at the patio door. No. That was impossible. Those had been illusions. Hallucinations from an overtired, stressed brain.

But what had killed Gracie?

The phone dinged. *Sorry about your cat.*

Fury raged through him. "You fuckers!" he screamed at the ceiling. He stomped through the house, rifling through stacks of books, nicknacks on shelves, knocking pictures askew and tipping over the lamp beside the sofa. Nothing out of the ordinary that he could see. "Where are they? Where are the cameras? I know you've got them around here somewhere."

A new text chimed in on his phone. *There are no cameras, Lee.*

"I will find you," he said, his voice even. "I will find you and I will make you pay for this."

He stood still as a stone, every hair on his body erect, his senses sharpened almost painfully by anger and fear. No sound but his own ragged breathing. His heart pounded in his chest, and his mouth was dry and tasted of old pennies.

The phone buzzed where he had tossed it on the sofa.

With a sinking feeling he peered down at it. Stared at the message. Felt his blood turn to ice.

Have you checked on Corey n Lizbeth?

He swiped up the phone, vaguely aware that he could barely feel his quaking fingers. "No!" he screamed. "Fuck, *no!*" He punched in the number of the house phone back in Springfield. After an eternity the warbled ringing on the other end began. He counted the rings. One. Two. Three. Four.

"Hello?" Corey. Thank God. Thank *God.*

"Hey, little man," Lee said, trying to disguise the terror in his voice. "Everything okay there?"

"We're okay," Corey said. "It's just dark. The power went out."

Oh, shit. If there was no power at the house that meant no heat. Everything was electric there. He'd always meant to install a generator, but it had been one of those things he'd never gotten around to. "You staying warm?"

"Kinda cold," Corey said. "Nana said if the power stays off, the three of us will have to sleep in the same bed in our clothes." He giggled. "Nana's wearing a hat."

"Corey, can I talk to Nana?"

"Yeah, hang on."

The phone thumped as Corey dropped it, and Lee could hear him calling Jessie's mother. Barbara finally answered, her voice high and strained. "Hey, Lee."

"How long has the power been out?"

"Since about two."

"Is it really cold in the house?"

"Thermostat says sixty-one."

Shit. "Well, you guys stay bundled up. I'm sure they'll get the power back on as soon as they can."

"It's still snowing here," Barbara said. "I haven't seen a snowplow since right before lunch. It's like they've just given up. I can't even tell where the street is anymore. It'll take *days* to dig out from all this." She lowered her voice to just above a whisper. "I'm kinda scared, Lee."

"I'm sure everything will be fine," he said, hoping it was true. He hesitated a moment, waiting for her to say she'd seen someone skulking about the house, or that she'd heard strange noises from deep in the walls. But she didn't. After an awkward silence, he said, "So have you heard anything else from Jessie today?"

"No," Barbara said, "but I'm sure she's busy, what with the storm and all."

"Yeah," Lee said. "I'm sure she is." He glanced about the living room, his eyes drawn to the shadowy corners. "The kids doing okay? They're not too much for you, are they?"

"They're fine," Barbara said. "Corey's still treating all this as a big adventure. And Lizbeth has finally accepted the fact that she has no internet. She's been reading all afternoon."

In spite of his fear, Lee felt a smile on his lips. "Is she close by? Can I talk to her?"

"Sure." He heard muffled voices as Barbara placed her hand over the receiver. Barbara calling Lizbeth, Lizbeth saying something back. Barbara's voice lower and insistent. Lizbeth's voice louder and high-pitched. After a moment, Barbara came back on the line. "I'm. . . sorry, Lee. She says she doesn't want to talk to you."

A pang of hurt stung his chest. "Oh. Okay."

"I'm sorry."

"It's okay, Barbara. It's not your fault."

"I don't know what's gotten into her."

"Don't worry about it." He sat down on the sofa.

"Listen. . . Barbara, you be careful over there."

"What? Why?"

Lee detected the fright in her voice and wished he hadn't said that. "Well, I don't want you to worry, but just stay. . . vigilant. With the power out and so much snow I just worry about people. . . doing things."

"This neighborhood's gated," Barbara said. "I'm not worried. Besides, no one's going to be sneaking around with this winter storm blowing through."

"True enough," Lee said. "All the alarms are on a battery backup, so you all should be safe. I just. . . worry." He thought about the text again: *Have you checked on Corey n Lizbeth?*

"Well, you wouldn't be much of a father if you didn't worry," Barbara said. She gave a laugh that sounded forced. A voice shrilled in the background, and Barbara said, "Corey wants to talk to you again."

Before Lee could say anything else, Corey was on the line. "Hey, Dad, how's your cat?"

Lee felt a sharp sting in his chest. "She's fine," he lied.

"Did she catch the mouse yet?"

"No, not yet."

"Did you – " Corey's voice faded into static.

"Corey?" Lee drew the phone back and looked at the screen. The call still showed connected. "Corey? Are you there?"

" – and then they disappeared."

"What? Who disappeared?"

"The people in the mirror."

Lee's eyes watered. "What people? What are you talking about?"

"The people in my mirror. They said – " More static.

"Corey? I can't hear you. You're breaking up. Corey?"

" – coming for you."

Lee's breath caught in his throat. "What? They said what? Who are you talking about?"

"Dad, can you hear me?"

"I'm right here, Corey. What were you saying?"

Silence. The phone beeped twice as the call dropped. Lee hit redial and waited for the connection.

Nothing. He checked the phone. No service. His heart sank. The cell tower must be out now. He set the phone down on the coffee table and sank onto the sofa. So now he was cut off from the kids. And from Jessie, if he believed Barbara that the internet was down all over Springfield. He wondered how long the service would be down. Whether it would come back up before his cell service did.

His laptop still sat on the dining table. He went to it and pressed the touchpad and the screen burst to life. He'd never turned it off, and he'd never logged off his email. Among the list of new messages was one from Jessie. He clicked on it.

From: Jessica Houston <jhouston@wspr-tv3.com>
To: Lee Houston <houston3@rronline.com>
Sent: Tuesday, January 10 9:56 AM
Subject: Hey

Wanted to touch base with you. I'm staying over at the station during this winter storm. Mom is with the kids. Things are supposed to get really bad. I hope you're ok down there.

I found the name of that guy that worked on the furnace. Chuck Heltsley. 270-555-3281. I tried calling him, but the number's been disconnected. Maybe you can track him down.

Something I wanted to talk to you about. And Lee, please don't get worried. Corey's been acting a little strange the last day or two since you've been away. He said something about seeing people in his room at night. The first time I thought maybe he'd just had a bad dream. But it happened Sunday night, too, and I talked to Mom and she said he mentioned it again when he got up this morning.

(*"The people in my mirror. . ."*)

Like I said, I don't want to worry you, but I just found it odd. He's never been one for "invisible friends" and all that. And he's never lied to us or made stuff up. Maybe it's just his way of coping with the stress of all that's going on with you and me. Anyway, you might want to call and talk to him. And Lizbeth, too. I think this is harder on her than she's letting on.

Hope you're getting some writing done down there. Love you and miss you.

Lee looked at the last sentence, feeling a pang of sadness and guilt. He searched somewhere within him for a hidden scrap of love for Jessie and found he had none; maybe if there were at least a shred of caring left the guilt wouldn't haunt him. Or maybe it would be worse. Maybe he had more love for her than he cared to admit. He wondered if she really meant what she said, or if it was just a way of signing off.

I'm glad you left me, you know.

But she'd said that in a dream. And a dream, no matter how real, was still just a dream. And if he tried to tell himself otherwise he would only be setting himself up for dancing on the edge of sanity.

But what about that disappearing wound on his chest? He had dreamed about that. Had woken up with a bleeding laceration that vanished as mysteriously as it appeared. Or the figures that had haunted him.

"The people in my mirror. . . "

He was sure he had dreamed *her*. Had hallucinated *him*. And yet he was conversing with them.

What was real? What was a dream? Had he already lost his mind just in the few short days he'd been here? And yet. . . the day he'd arrived here – excited and content to be alone for a while – seemed months ago. And weeks since his night with Kat. And his phone conversations with her and Bill and Harvey. . . had that just been this morning?

He looked back at the email from Jessie. *I don't want to worry you.* He tapped out a quick reply: Things are going good here. Getting a lot accomplished. I wouldn't worry too much about Corey. I'm sure he's just having dreams about something he saw on TV. Glad you're staying at the station where it's safe.

He stared at his response, wondering why he was lying to her. Nothing he said to her was the truth. And yet, he couldn't bring himself to say what he wanted. He would sound insane if he did.

He read the reply once more, then added: My cell service is down out here but I still have internet. Barbara said everything is out in Springfield, but if by some chance you still have access to your email let me know. Right now this is the only way I can communicate with anyone. He hit send and watched the message disappear from his outbox, then closed the laptop.

The world beyond the patio doors was black and featureless. He could only see himself reflected in the glass, illuminated by the undercabinet lights from the kitchen. God, he looked awful. Emaciated and pale. Almost like a corpse.

He hobbled to the living room and turned on the TV. Maybe he could find a weather report to at least see when the storm would pass. But there was nothing on the screen but a message reading "Loss of signal – Call to report a problem." He stabbed the "off" button in frustration. Damn. The satellite dish on the roof must be buried in snow. He snapped on the radio sitting on the bookshelf where he'd knocked it askew earlier, but there was nothing but static. He ran up and down the dial. Nothing. Were all the stations in the area without power now? He flipped the switch to AM and turned the knob slowly until he caught a murmur of a voice through the crackling hum, faint and barely intelligible.

" . . .and we'll continue to keep you updated as this substantial blizzard moves across America's heartland. Right now many cities in the Midwest are without power, and most communication services are down. If you're hearing us now, that means you're one of the lucky ones who still has electricity or you were prepared and have a battery-powered radio. Here at the station we're running on our back-up generator until we can get power restored, but we're doing all we can to keep you informed of how things are progressing here in the Chicago area."

He blinked. *Chicago*? That was almost seven hours away. He moved the dial up and down, but there was nothing else coming through. And when he returned to the spot where he'd heard the ghostly voice from Illinois, it too had vanished into a hiss of static. He snapped off the radio. This storm must be massive.

He righted the books he'd smacked off the shelf and replaced the bric-a-brac – souvenirs from vacations and day-trips mostly – and limped back to the dining room. He fell into the chair at the table and opened the laptop. The screen was still pulled up to his email, but there was no response from Jessie.

He opened his browser and navigated to the TV station's website again. The page was dominated by a photograph of downtown Springfield buried beneath at least two feet of snow. The streets – or what he presumed were the streets – were empty and lifeless. Drifts covered storefronts almost to the tops of the display windows. He wondered how anyone had managed to wade into the street to snap the picture until he read the caption: *North Main Street as captured by our First State Bank WeatherCam.*

He scrolled down the page to the headlines. "Blizzard Paralyzes Nation." And below that, "Springfield Mayor Declares Disaster; Snowplows

Unable to Leave City Garage."

A map below the stories showed the immense storm stretching from the middle of Texas into Canada and from Missouri to the Atlantic Coast. There would be snow for at least one more day.

Damn. Everything was pretty well fucked. He could only hope Barbara and the kids would be safe, that they could stay warm enough until the power was restored. He wasn't worried about Jessie; if the station was still updating its website, chances are they were running on generators, just like the radio station he'd picked up in Chicago. And Kat said she was fine. And he was good with plenty of firewood and a stockpile of food. There was nothing to do now but wait it out.

His phone dinged again with an incoming message, and he grabbed it. The cell tower must be back online.

Hi Lee

Fuck. "What do you want now?" he said, his voice a hollow ring through the house. He looked back at the screen.

No signal.

But that was impossible. They must be using some kind of anonymous booster signal or something that hid itself from his phone. And the cameras and microphones hidden in the house must be some kind of tiny wireless gear. He'd researched that for one of the Max Plexico books. He wondered where the assholes were hiding, and guessed they were probably in one of the empty summer houses. Maybe even the Millers'. Shit, they'd most likely watched him walk up to the house and peer into the windows, followed him through the woods like wolves. Maybe even killed the deer.

But what about Gracie? She couldn't have done that

to herself. Something had come into the house and attacked her. Maybe the thing gnawing in the walls. And maybe that had nothing to do with whoever this was fucking with him.

But somehow he knew better.

What he couldn't figure out was why. If they were stalkers, they were nothing like Cameron Fields. Cameron was troubled for sure. But in the end, he'd only wanted to get close to Lee. Somehow he'd seen Lee as a close friend; maybe even a surrogate father. These people seemed bent only on tormenting him. What did they want? Money? Or were they just getting their rocks off fucking around with him? And why pretend to be Nicky and Carly of all people? And how were they getting into the house?

And they had to have been in the house. To set up cameras and microphones. To appear at the foot of his bed. To kill poor Gracie.

Right?

But he had searched every inch of this place and seen nothing. No evidence whatsoever that anyone had been here except himself. None of it made any sense.

But then nothing at all had made much sense since he'd arrived here. Disappearing wounds. Dead deer carcasses. Invisible creatures gnawing somewhere within the bowels of the house. Pleading hands reaching from the black waters of the lake.

Just a broken tree branch, bobbing in the current.

No. It wasn't. He knew what he'd seen. Just as he knew what he'd seen standing at the foot of his bed. And on the deck outside the patio doors.

Whoever this was knew what had happened to Nicky and Carly. And they knew Nicky's body had washed up next to Lee's boat dock.

A thought struck him. Harvey. Could Harvey have something to do with this? After all, Harvey knew he was here alone. Knew he was isolated. Knew Corey and Lizbeth and Jessie's names. And Harvey knew the details of Nicky's death.

But again, why? What possible reason could a seventy-something-year-old coot have to try to scare the bejesus out of him?

On a whim, he turned to the browser on his laptop and typed in *Nick Compton drowning Harper's Lake*. A list of articles presented themselves, but none seemed to address Nicky's death directly. One item near the bottom of the page drew his attention. *Tragedy and Sorrow: The Sad Tale of Harper's Lake*. He clicked on it.

> Near the southwestern tip of the state, nestled among pine-covered hills, sits the tiny resort community of Harper's Lake. During the summer months the town's public beaches are swarming with day-trippers and folks who make the area their home during the hot, humid days between Memorial Day and Labor Day. Folks the locals refer to as "summer people from 'away.'"
>
> But many visitors are unaware as they swim in the water and skim across its surface in boats and on skis of the town's dark past, and a history that is scarred by tragedy and heartbreak.

Altogether a total of 127 people have died in the roiling waters of Harper's Lake since 1893. Of that number, only two bodies have ever been recovered. The first reported death, and for many decades the only body to be fished from the lake, was Miss Ellie Lavonne Majors, a 17-year-old debutant from Nashville, Tennessee, who in a state of inconsolable depression intentionally drowned herself by leaping from the now-demolished Smith's Pier on the west side of the lake on August 6, 1893. Upon the recovery of her body, it was rumored she was pregnant by a local innkeeper, 53-year-old Simon Jeffries, with whom she'd been seen socially. The rumor was never confirmed and Jeffries was never questioned; his empty fishing boat was discovered abandoned near the center of the lake three days later, and Jeffries was never heard from again. It was speculation at the time that Jeffries set his boat adrift from the shore and fled town to avoid implication in Miss Majors' death, but in the wake of more deaths over the next century some people believe Jeffries followed Ellie's lead and flung himself overboard.

Boating mishaps, automobile accidents, suicides, murders. . . tragedy seemed to flourish over the years at Harper's Lake. Perhaps the most infamous death on the water occurred in the winter of 1929 when Hollywood actor Charles Preston drove his Rolls-Royce roadster out to the middle of the ice-covered lake as a publicity stunt. Ignoring warnings of thin ice, Preston convinced several in his entourage to join him, including a photographer from *Motion Picture Magazine* who was hired to record the outing for posterity. As the group approached the center of the lake, with Preston driving the car and the others following him, the ice suddenly gave way beneath them, plunging them all into the frigid black water. Neither Preston nor the people accompanying him nor the Rolls-Royce were ever recovered.

Many experts believe the extreme depth of the lake – 698 feet – makes the recovery of bodies difficult, though ask a few locals and they'll tell you there is a less scientific and more supernatural reason.

"The water's cursed," says 82-year-old Ed Zimmerman, a lifelong resident of Harper's Lake. "The Indians did it, right before they got drove out by the federal government." Zimmerman is of course referring to resettlement of Native Americans during the Andrew Jackson administration's Indian Removal Policy in 1838-39 and what became known as the Trail of Tears. "The Indians said if they couldn't have the big waters, the *equa ama*, then no one could have it. I still won't eat any fish you catch out there. All those bodies that have disappeared over the years, you know those fish been eating on them."

Curses or not, Harper's Lake three-term mayor Ben Settle says the area's tourism is at an all-time high. "People love it here. There are some families who've been coming here for generations. They don't go anywhere else. Not Florida, not the east coast, not Mexico. They love Harper's Lake. They remember coming here as little kids, and now they want to experience the fun with their own children."

Perhaps the curse of Harper's Lake has finally been broken. The last drowning was over twenty years ago, ironically almost exactly a century to the day since Ellie Lavonne Majors took her fatal plunge. It was also the only other body ever recovered from the waters. A boating accident claimed the lives of Nicholas Compton and his girlfriend, Carly Sievers, on August 10, 1993. While Carly's body was never found, Nicholas' body washed ashore near Glen Cove Road. There have been no fatalities on the water since.

It was as if the lake said, "I've had enough."

Lee sat staring at the screen, his skin prickled with gooseflesh.

I've had enough.

He shivered. The article was dated almost two years ago, and he wondered if there had been any deaths since. Somehow he doubted it. Somehow it seemed the writer of the article may have been correct. The lake had consumed all it wanted.

In the browser he typed *Harper's Lake drownings* and browsed through the results. Nothing but the same articles he'd seen from his previous search. He changed *"drownings"* to *"deaths"* and hit "Search." At the top of the page was what he'd been looking for: *Harper's Lake Man Dies in Boating Accident*. The article was from the archives of the Cedar Hill *Post-Dispatch* and was dated August 10, 1993:

> A Harper's Lake man died Sunday afternoon when the boat he was in capsized during a heavy thunderstorm.
>
> According to friends, Nicholas Compton, 22, and his girlfriend Carly Sievers, also 22, had just left a gathering on the north shore of Harper's Lake in an effort to beat the storm back to Compton's family home on the south side of the lake. Lake County Water Patrol discovered Compton's boat capsized late Sunday night but found no sign of either Compton or Sievers.
>
> Compton's body was found washed ashore Monday morning not far from his

family's home. Sievers is still missing.
"We're going to keep looking for her,"
Sheriff Paul Cotton said. "This is still very
much a rescue operation."

In the search bar, Lee typed in *"Nicholas Compton obituary"* and waited for the results to load. But nothing he read shed any light on Nicky's death. He had just started to close out of the browser when something at the bottom of the page caught his eye. He read through it, his heart thudding dully in his chest, not believing what he was seeing. He clicked on the full article.

Police Investigate Harper's Lake Man's Death

Police were called to a residence on Glen
Cove Road in Harper's Lake Thursday to
investigate the death of a local man after
his body was discovered by a neighbor.

Authorities say Harvey Gene Compton,
73, died as a result of a gunshot wound to
the head that did not appear to be
accidental. No further investigation into the
death is expected.

Lee checked the date of the article. November. He leaned back in the chair, his eyes still glued to the screen.

If Harvey Compton had been dead since November, then who the fuck was living in his house pretending to be him?

In the search bar he typed *Harvey Compton*

Harper's Lake obituary and hit enter.

One single hit from Shepherd's Memorial Chapel in Harper's Lake. He clicked on it.

Harvey Gene Compton, 73

Harvey Gene Compton, 73, of Glen Cove Road, Harper's Lake, died November 3 at his residence.

A graveside service will be held Tuesday, November 10 at 2:00 PM in Oak Grove Cemetery. There will be no visitation.

Mr. Compton was preceded in death by his wife Gail in 2009 and his son Nicholas Wayne in 1993.

A chill settled over him, prickling his skin to gooseflesh, and his eyes watered. The obituary was accompanied by a single photograph of a white-haired man wearing denim bib overalls, a tan Carhartt jacket, and a John Deere cap. It was Harvey. The Harvey that had first spoken to him in the front yard on Saturday. The same Harvey that had sat at this very table drinking coffee. No doubt about it.

The laptop screen suddenly went black, and Lee was left alone with deafening silence and impenetrable darkness.

The power was out.

IV

Darkness Dawn

FOR A MOMENT, all Lee could do was sit in the inky blackness, the silence crushing him like a vise. Then little by little his vision began to adjust to the gray light beyond the patio doors. He eased himself from the table and shuffled toward it, feeling his way around the dining chairs, until his fingertips touched the cold glass.

Outside was nothing but a murky, colorless haze. The deck railing was a vague darker shape, and the only feature he could make out. He could just barely see the snow still sifting down, silent and steady as ashes.

It was the quiet that was unnerving. No rattling hum of the refrigerator or drone of the furnace. No whir of the fan from his laptop. Even the wind had ceased.

Nothing. Nothing but the thudding of his own heartbeat in his ears.

There was a flash of light behind him and a chime. His phone. An incoming text. And it wasn't hard to guess who it was from. He felt his way toward the glow and grabbed up the phone.

Dark ain't it

He blew out a breath. He'd had it with these fuckers. He was just going to ignore them. He switched on the phone's flashlight and made his way to the living room. With the power out, the house was going to get cold quickly. He wanted to start a fire and at least keep warm. He thought fleetingly of the food in the refrigerator, and decided if nothing else he could set it all outside on the deck in the snow to keep it from spoiling. It wasn't the best choice, but it would have to do.

By the dim glow of the phone's LED, he stacked logs and kindling sticks in the fireplace, then crumpled up a few pages he ripped from a three-year-old issue of *House Beautiful* and set the whole thing ablaze with a match, then opened the flue. In a few moments the kindling caught and flames licked the thick logs above, filling the room with the pulsating glow. He sat back on the sofa, staring into the fire, mesmerized by the crackle. The earthy odor of the burning wood was intoxicating, evoking memories of camping as a scout. Of Christmases when Lizbeth and Corey were little. Of a million things when he was happy. When he and Jessie still gave a damn. The heat surrounded him, cuddling him like a blanket, and he wondered why he hadn't done this days ago. Why he had suffered in the damp chill of the house and the fickle furnace when all he'd had to do was build a fire.

The quiet and the darkness and the warmth were a rapid sedative, and he found himself drowsy within minutes, his eyelids heavy, his mind cloudy with racing

thoughts. The lake. Gracie. He and Cory chasing the
fireflies. Jessie's eyes tearing up as he packed. Kat and
the magical evening they'd had. The deer carcass on the
lake trail. Harvey.

His eyes snapped open. It couldn't be. The man he
knew as Harvey was a flesh-and-blood person. They'd
shaken hands, and Lee remembered the feel of
Harvey's callused skin against his own. Hell, Lee had
smelled him for chrissakes. A mixture of old work
sweat and stale after shave. And now what? He was
supposed to believe the person he knew was a fucking
ghost?

This couldn't be real. That man who'd been here,
whom Lee had entertained and talked with on the
phone, was an imposter. Someone made up to look like
the real Harvey. Someone in a conspiracy with whoever
the hell had been fucking with him since he got here.

He looked around in the flickering darkness. "Are
you still watching me? Can you hear me?"

His phone dinged: *Yes*.

He blew out a breath. "Okay, then. Joke's over. Ha,
ha, ha. You've had your fun. Can you just leave me
alone now please?"

The phone buzzed in his hand. *The fun's just gettin
started Lee*.

Rage ballooned inside him. "What do you want from
me? Money? You want money? Is that it?"

We don't want your money Lee

"Then what do you want?" He was aware his voice
was becoming higher-pitched as his exasperation grew,
and he was helpless to stop it. And that's what they
wanted. They wanted him scared and frustrated and
angry. This was their game. And he had to figure out

some way to stop playing. Maybe if he just ignored them, just stopped reacting.

The phone chimed: *Come join us Lee*

He powered off the phone and set it on the coffee table. He stared into the flickering flames, trying to disregard the burning he felt deep within his bowels. He should have turned the phone off earlier, when he first lost the signal. He never should have talked to them, never should have acknowledged them.

He thought back to what Dr. Thayer had told him in those therapy sessions in that spartan office in Springfield. Dr. Thayer with his round glasses and pointy Van Dyke beard, like some caricature, some goddamned actor playing the part of a psychoanalyst. "You are in control, Lee. You have to power to decide how you react. It's your choice whether to engage. If you feel someone is baiting you, don't engage. It really is that simple."

Don't engage. He should have heeded that advice earlier.

"I'm done," he said aloud to the darkness. "I'm through playing with you. Whoever you are."

He sat stiff and tense for a moment, expecting. . . he didn't know what. Something to swim up from the dark to claim him? That unearthly gnawing from within the walls of the house? But there was nothing. The crackling of the fire. The faint whisper of the wind outside the cabin. The occasional creak and pop as the wooden frame of the house settled and contracted from the cold. He let a long breath escape him. Felt his muscles relax a little. Even if they could still hear him, even if they could still see him through their cameras, they couldn't talk to him. Couldn't text him. Couldn't engage him.

Then, just as he began to feel the mesmerizing pull of the flickering flames again, he heard a shrill jingle from deep within the bowels of the house. A telephone. Somewhere upstairs. And he remembered – the landline Jessie had insisted they maintain in case of an emergency. He'd forgotten all about it. Hadn't thought about it in years, actually, and since Jessie always paid the bills, he never had reason to.

He knew who was calling. And he knew the ringing would continue until he answered it, or until he tore the cord from the wall.

He powered on his phone and switched on the LED to light his way through the darkness toward the sound above. The blue-white light barely penetrated the blackness before him as he climbed the stairs, and he was reminded of the old video from the 'eighties, of the remote broadcast of the robot in the ballroom of the sunken *Titanic*, and how as the camera snaked through the inky darkness, waltzing ghosts seemed just out of sight, just beyond the reach of the light. Gooseflesh prickled his neck, and a sudden chill rippled through him. It was already much colder up here; he would sleep in the living room tonight in front of the fire.

The telephone continued ringing from the other end of the hallway. He traced the sound to the spare bedroom in the back of the house and swung open the door. Any icy blast of air washed over him. The bed lay still and perfectly made, not one crease in the floral spread. He'd checked this room already, of course, but he hadn't noticed the old red plastic handset on the nightstand in the corner. A relic from the early 'nineties. He moved around the bed, barking his kneecap on the footboard. The pain barely registered. All he could focus on was the incessant ringing of the damned phone.

He stood looking at it as it continued to jingle. A metallic, mechanical shrill. A sound he was sure Lizbeth and Corey had never heard outside of a movie or a "vintage" ringtone on a smartphone. He should just unplug it. Rip the cord from the wall, wrap it around the handset and leave it. Or toss it out into the snow.

But he knew he couldn't. He knew he would answer it, for whatever reason. He reached for the receiver and lifted it. The ringing ceased and died away. He put the headset against his ear and heard nothing. Dead air. Not even the hum of electricity through the wires. His voice came out as a faint whisper as he said, "Hello?"

For a moment there was only silence through the earpiece. Then came the low rumble of a masculine chuckle. And he recognized the laugh. He'd heard it downstairs in his kitchen, and outside in his yard. Fingers of ice traced down his spine. "Harvey?"

"How ya doing, son? You staying warm down there?"

Lee's fear gave way to sudden anger. "Who is this? I know you're not Harvey. The real Harvey Compton is dead. I don't know what you people want, or why you're doing this, but leave me the fuck alone. This game or whatever it is – it's over."

"Now, why are you getting so riled up, Lee?" Harvey said. "You really should just calm down. Come on out and join us. There's a whole mess of us waiting."

Lee's anger was dissolving into a blind rage. He felt the physical transformation in his gut and chest, an intoxicating burning. "Waiting for what? What the fuck are you talking about? When this storm is over, I'm calling the sheriff."

Harvey laughed, an ear-splitting guffaw. "Lee, you poor deluded son-of-a-gun. You can't arrest the dead."

Lee shook his head. "You know, this isn't funny. Never was. I don't know what kind of bad movies you people have been watching, but you obviously haven't learned much."

"Look outside, Lee," Harvey said, all traces of humor gone from his gravelly voice. "Go on. Look."

The gooseflesh was back on Lee's neck. "Why?"

"Look!"

Lee moved toward the lone window in the room and brushed aside the drapes. In better weather there was a view of the dock and the lake, of the town across the water. But now, as he expected, there was nothing but the darkish-gray mass of the winter night, the barely perceptible flutter of a snowflake or two as – finally – the storm seem to have abated. And something else. He pushed his face against the glass, telling himself he couldn't possibly be seeing what he imagined.

There were people out there. Dozens. Standing between the deck and and the slope down to the water. Not moving. Just standing. Watching the house. Watching *him*. But that was impossible. The snow was at least two feet deep, and the figures were *on top* of it. And in all manner of dress. T-shirts and shorts. Swimsuits. Jeans and sweatshirts. Suits and ties. A man in a tuxedo. And a woman in a dress that ballooned out from her waist to her feet; her hair was disheveled and matted, but he knew who she was immediately: Ellie Majors.

His stomach was a vat of acid, the bile rising in his throat. This couldn't be. It couldn't be. It was the ones the lake had claimed. All of them.

Their eyes were gone, replaced with black voids, the fleshy orbs long ago eaten away by turtles and lake trout.

A lone figure moved through the others, edging closer to the house. Lee knew it was Harvey; he recognized the John Deere cap and overalls. He spoke, and his voice came not from the body standing out in the snow but from the receiver pressed against Lee's ear. "We're all waiting, Lee. It will be so much easier if you just come out and join us."

Lee realized he was gripping the phone so tightly that his fingers had become numb. "Go to hell," he croaked.

Harvey looked up directly at him, and for the first time Lee noticed one side of the man's face was gone. Obliterated. Blown away by a shotgun blast two months ago. Ragged lips stretched over what was left of Harvey's jagged teeth. He smiled. "Kat's here with us."

Lee froze. "What?"

And suddenly, there she was, threading her way through the maze of the stone-like crowd. Wearing a stained white t-shirt and panties. Her feet were bare, and he could see her erect nipples pressing against the shirt. She smiled up at him, her face sallow and gaunt, and her voice crackled through the receiver like dry leaves. "You were always up for a good fuck, Lee."

He stared in horror at Kat's sunken features. Her listless hair, her blotchy skin. "No," he whispered.

"You don't remember, do you?" she said. "You really don't!" She laughed – a heavy, breathless rasp.

"Oh, fuck me, this is rich!"

His whole body throbbed. He looked at the gathering below as if he were viewing it on a television screen. It wasn't real. None of it was real. "No!"

He slammed the receiver into the phone's cradle and yanked the cord from the wall. "No!"

Blindly, he stumbled out of the room and down the hall toward the stairs. He could see the flickering firelight from the living room below. Somewhere he had lost his phone and his source of light, but it didn't matter. He tripped on the top step and tumbled halfway down the stairs. Something snapped in his hip. His thigh went numb, then blossomed with pain. For a moment he could only lie frozen in agony, his breath shallow and fast. His leg was broken. He knew it. He pulled himself the rest of the way down to the warmth of the living room.

The bookshelf at the foot of the stairs seemed a mile away, but he managed to crawl to it. On the bottom shelf was a set of old encyclopedias. He pawed at them, and they fell from the case. Behind them in the dim flickering light he saw a slim volume with a gray cover. A handsome hardcover book that he remembered hiding here from Jessie two summers ago. On the front, a soft black-and-white portrait of Kat, and below her photograph *The Collected Poetry of Kat Cunningham.* How could he have forgotten? How had he not remembered until now? He flipped to the back flap of the dustjacket and read the copy with fascination and horror:

ABOUT THE AUTHOR
Kat Cunningham won many awards

for her poetry during her short career, including the prestigious Lifetime Achievement Medal given post-humously by the American Poetry Foundation. Ms. Cunningham died in 2010.

The book slid from Lee's grasp and landed on the floor with a thud. He stared at it, at Kat's face on the cover, at the sadness in her faint smile. The accusatory glint in her gaze.

You were always up for a good fuck, Lee.

The memory hit him like a punch to the jaw. Kat in his bed. His and Jessie's bed. The one upstairs here in this house. Kat naked, covered only in a white sheet up to her shoulders. A lone tear streaming from the corner of one eye down to the pillow as she stared at the ceiling. Her voice cracking as she said it. *You were always up for a good fuck, Lee.*

And himself, standing next to the bed, shirtless, pulling up his jeans. Watching her and feeling a quiet loathing where just an hour before he'd felt passion and longing. His own voice, cold and distant. *We both knew this could never work.*

The lake a dull shimmer outside the bedroom window. A lone fisherman in a yellow rain slicker out on the water in a small boat in the rain. And it *was* raining. The drops pattered against the glass in a staccato rhythm. The light played against them, forming shadows on Kat's face, and as the droplets ran down the pane, their shadow-ghosts ran down Kat's cheeks.

A chance encounter. That's what it had been. He'd been passing through Cedar Hill on his way home from a regional book convention. The second Max Plexico book was just out, and Circle had sent him out on a one-man show to promote it. Not much of a budget, but in those days no one knew what an impact ol' Max was going to make in the young adult literature world. Jessie had called him on his way home. They needed cat litter, she said, and he told her he would stop at the pet store in Cedar Hill because he wanted to see if they had those little furry mice Macbeth enjoyed so much.

He saw her in the cat food aisle. He spoke to her. She dropped a can of Friskies. She stooped to retrieve it but it rolled beneath the shelf and they stared at each other and laughed. She was teaching freshman comp at the college, she said, having just moved from Seattle. He asked to join her at her usual Monday hangout, a little coffee shop just off campus where she went to write, just to catch up. Reluctantly she agreed. She told him about her failed marriage to the music producer and moving back to find herself and start over. He told her about his and Jessie's troubles, which at the time were just beginning. They ended up at Kat's apartment, making frantic love while her white cat watched from where it perched atop the lingerie chest. Afterward, Kat cried. She told him how much she'd missed him, and how much she wished things had been different. He told her he still loved her.

His Monday visits to Cedar Hill became a regular occurrence, and when spring blossomed that year, they took to meeting at the lake house. More privacy, he told her. They could be loud. And she laughed at that. Once, daringly, they made love on the deck in full view of the lake, grinding on an old doubled up blanket he found in the closet. Most weeks he left early so he could be home before Jessie came in from work, and Kat stayed the rest of the day and usually overnight. She enjoyed the serenity of the lake, she said, and it was conducive to bringing out her creativity.

While Lee never thought Jessie knew what was happening, he became paranoid that she suspected something. On their weekend visits to the lake, he spent the entire time fearful Jessie would find some misplaced item of Kat's – a pair of panties, an old lipstick, a wadded receipt from an anonymous ATM. And finally, on a hot, sultry morning in mid-July it happened.

A Sunday morning. They'd just awoken, and Lee had gone downstairs to start the coffee. He peeled off the plastic lid and stared into the can. The grounds were crawling with small white worms. At some point the container must not have been sealed completely, and some kind of insect had crawled inside to lay eggs. Disgusted, he threw the entire can into the garbage. Behind him, he heard Jessie shuffling into the kitchen. "Bad news," he said. "The coffee's got worms in it. I'll throw on some clothes and go to town. Anything else we need while I'm there?" He looked up at her and froze. Her face was flushed and harsh. "What's wrong?"

She lifted her hand and held it out to him. She was holding a prescription bottle. "What is this?"

He took it from her and read Kat's name. A prescription for Ativan. He looked into her blazing glare. "I can explain," he said, feeling the blood drain from his limbs. "It's not what it looks like."

"What does it look like?" she said, her voice devoid of any inflection.

"Kat's been staying here some," he said. "She comes here to write."

Jessie was shaking her head. "Why? Why would you let your old girlfriend stay at our house?"

"I didn't think it was a big deal."

Jessie's voice finally broke. "Why didn't you discuss this with me first?" She closed her eyes and turned away. "God, I'm so stupid. How long has this been going on?"

Lee took a step toward her, his hand caught between touching her shoulder and yanking her around to face him. "You mean, how long has she been coming here and writing?"

Jessie whirled to look at him. Tears were coursing down her face. "The affair, Lee. How long have you been seeing her behind my back?"

He did touch her then, noticing how she flinched when his fingertips brushed her arm. "There is no affair," he said, feeling bile rise in his throat as he lied. "She just comes here to write. I swear."

"Why were these pills in our bedroom? Is she sleeping in there?"

He shook his head. "I don't know. I guess. I didn't ask her."

"End it," Jessie said. Her rage had turned cold and her voice was back to being emotionless. And somehow this scared him more. "Whatever this is," she said, "it stops now. I don't want her in this house anymore. And if you're cheating on me, we're done. Understand? Get rid of her or we're through, Lee. I'm not fucking around."

She turned and headed back up the stairs, and from where he stood like a stone he could hear her crying in the bedroom. His whole body was numb.

The rest of the day they avoided each other, and the ride back to Springfield was silent and tense. Neither Lizbeth or Corey seemed to notice, and for that he was grateful. That night he stayed in the guest bedroom for the first time, and when he awoke in the morning to the sound of thunder, Jessie had already left for work. Today he would end things with Kat. As much as he still loved her, he couldn't do this to Jessie.

Jessie's mother arrived around nine, her usual time, to care for the kids while school was out so Lee could work. She'd never questioned Lee's Monday outings for "research," and as he left that morning he wondered if Jessie would tell her what she'd discovered. Somehow he doubted it; Jessie kept most things private, even from her mother. Even from herself.

When Lee pulled up at the cabin an hour later, he found Kat already there. She'd evidently already been writing; her laptop was set up on the dining room table facing the rainswept lake, and a half-drunk cup of coffee sat next to it. "Kat?"

"Up here," she called from the bedroom. He mounted the steps and found her naked in the bed. She giggled playfully. "You know how storms make me horny."

He stepped toward her. "Look, baby, I – "

He was interrupted by a roll of thunder. Kat squealed and leapt from beneath the covers. Her breasts swung, her nipples erect. She grabbed him and pulled him toward the bed, planting her lips on his. Her fingers flew down his shirt, unleashing the buttons, then lower to rub him through his jeans. In spite of everything, he was growing stiff with want. He wriggled out of his shirt, his mouth still working hungrily on hers, then quickly shed the rest of his clothes. She pulled him down to the bed, and as the thunder roared outside and the rain pounded the window, they made love. No, he thought as they were doing it. It wasn't making love. They were going at it like animals. This was sex for the pleasure of sex. Primal and emotionless. This was *fucking*. They were fucking like mindless rabbits, and he hated himself for doing it. Hated himself because even though he came here to end it, he wanted one last fuck. One last orgasm with her.

And when they were done, both covered in tepid, viscous sweat, he rolled off her, panting, and stared at the beams of the ceiling. Already he was awash with guilt and shame. She curled against him, and he felt his liquid seeping from her against his leg, cold and slick. Her hand ruffled the hair across his chest, and he took it, interlacing her fingers with his own. She kissed his shoulder, then traced her lips down to his nipple and nibbled it gently with her teeth, sending a jolt of pleasure through him. "Stop," he said.

She giggled and did it again. "Oh yeah? You want me to stop?"

He looked at her. "Yes. Stop it."

She drew back and stared at him. "What's wrong? Did I hurt you?"

He sat up, rubbing his temples as the sheet fell to his waist. "We need to talk."

"What's the matter?" He could hear alarm in her voice, and for some reason it angered him. She flopped back onto her pillow. "I know that tone," she said, and laughed bitterly. "This is where it all ends, isn't it?"

"Kat – "

"You're finally tired of me and now it's over." She snorted. "It's okay, Lee. I'm a big girl. I've been through this before, you know."

"Jessie found your bottle of Ativan," he said, not looking at her. "It was under the bed. I guess you dropped it the last time you were here."

She laughed, and he detected a viciousness he'd never heard before. "I didn't drop it," she said. "I left it there on purpose."

He stared at her, letting her words ferment. "You *what*? Why?"

"It was time she knew, Lee."

Rage boiled within him. Rage and fear. All mixed up. "Why would you do such a thing? I had to convince her you were just coming here to write, that there was nothing going on between us. Why would you screw this up? *Why*?"

"Because I love you!" she screamed. She looked at him only a moment before covering her face in her hands and sobbing. "I love you, Lee. I want to be with you. Always."

"You know that's not possible," he whispered.

"I just thought…if that hateful bitch knew about us, that she'd leave you. That we could be together again." He watched as spittle flew from her mouth when she said the word "bitch."

"We've talked about this before," he said. He reached for her arm and she jerked it away.

"Don't touch me!" she spat. "Don't!"

He shook his head and slid out of the bed. "Look, Kat. We had fun for a while. But we knew all along how it was going to end."

Kat reached down and pulled the sheet up to cover

her breasts. "I should have known," she said. "But I didn't. I guess I have just enough naiveté to think you wanted something more from me than just a fuck." She stared at the ceiling. One lone tear leaked from the corner of her eye. "But you were always up for a good fuck, Lee." Her face was colorless in the gray light from the window, and the rain droplets sliding down the glass made shadows on her cheeks. Tears within tears. Suddenly he hated her. Hated that she had tricked him. Had pulled that stunt with the pill bottle.

He stepped into his jeans and slid them up his thighs. "We both knew this could never work." He fastened the button and something out on the water caught his attention. A lone fisherman in a small boat. Clad in a bright yellow rainslicker. He had just enough time wonder why the damn fool was out on the lake in the middle of a monsoon when Kate erupted with a shriek.

She flew from beneath the sheet, her dark hair wild and matted from their lovemaking, her brown eyes black and filled with rage, her scream slicing through his ears like a knife. She hit him full force, and they fell to the floor with a thump that rattled a small vase off the chest in the corner. She continued to scream, her eyes wild with madness, her face inches from his.

He was gasping with pain. *Knocked the breath out of me*, some lingering rational part of his brain thought. He groped for a handhold to pull himself out from under her, to get her off his chest so he could breathe. He had to breathe! With all his remaining strength, he pushed against her shoulders, knocking her off balance. She rolled off to the side and tried to catch herself. But her head banged against the oak rail of the bed. She fell backwards. Unconscious. And that's when he saw the yellow-handled screwdriver as it fell from her hand and clattered to the floor. The tip of its chrome shaft was covered in blood, and the first thought in his mind was that she'd jabbed herself when they fell.

Then the pain exploded in his chest and he knew. He glanced down and saw the dark blood flowing from a jagged wound just off center between his nipples. Already it was dripping to the floor beneath him. His fingers found the gash and pressed against it. They were shaking, and he realized his hands were going numb. And that same small sentient part of his mind was whispering *shock. Shock. Shock.* The word resounded through his brain as if spoken in an echo chamber.

The phone. He had to get to the phone before he passed out.

He untangled his legs from Kat's and pulled himself across the floor toward the nightstand. Each inch across the hardwood seemed a mile. He could see the red phone sitting there next to a small lamp. The lamp, he remembered crazily, he'd found in an antique shop here at Harper's Lake. It was brass, and the shade was an off-white. He grasped the cord of the phone and pulled it off the nightstand. It landed next to his face on the floorboards with a harsh clang of the bells inside. He could hear the dim hum of the dial tone. He pressed 9-1-1 and lay his head down on his arm. He was aware of someone speaking through the receiver, but he had neither the strength nor the words to answer. All he knew was he wanted to sleep. His eyelids were heavy.

So heavy. . .

* * *

The first thing he was aware of was the weight of the blanket on top of him. There was a beeping – steady and piercing. And gray light filtering through his eyelids. And when he opened them, he saw he was in a hospital room. The blinds on the window were shut, and a dim light above his bed was the only source of light. Jessie sat beside him in a chair, her eyes closed and her head slumped forward. She was dozing, and he wondered what time it was and how long he'd been here. He reached out for her, but his arm was caught by the IV lines. He lay his head back on the pillow. "Jessie?" he croaked, and his throat felt like sandpaper.

Jessie's eyelids fluttered open, and she gave him a weak smile. "You're awake." She reached out and took his hand, and her fingers were smooth and warm.

"How long have I been out?"

"You've been here for two days," she said. "Do you remember what happened?"

He looked down at his chest. He was wrapped in gauze and bandages from his armpits to his navel. "Kat. . ."

Jessie nodded.

He tried to sit up, but Jessie held him down. "She attacked me. She had a screwdriver."

Jessie pushed his shoulders gently back down to the bed. "It's all right, Lee. Everything is fine. The screwdriver punctured your lung and just nicked your heart, but you're going to be all right."

"But she's – "

"She's dead, Lee."

He stared at her. He'd heard her words, but they seemed to have no meaning. *She's dead. Dead, dead, dead, dead.* And he realized he was speaking the word aloud.

Jessie was nodding, and tears spilled down her

cheeks. "Yes. She overdosed on painkillers and antidepressants."

Lee flattened against the bed. All his strength had escaped him like air from a balloon. "She's dead."

"She left a note. They didn't find her until yesterday morning. She left the lake and went back to her apartment, took the pills and got in the tub. They think she actually drowned."

He stared at the tiled ceiling, at the unlit fluorescent lights. "She's dead," he said again.

"Her note told everything that happened, at least her side of it." Jessie took his hand again and squeezed it. "I'm sorry, baby. I know. . . " She closed her eyes and more tears rolled down her face. "I know you still had feelings for her." She lifted his hand to her lips and kissed it. "The police will want to talk with you when you're feeling stronger. But they said – "

"Go home, Jessie," he said, not looking at her.

He felt her stiffen, and she let go of his hand. "You. . . want me to leave?"

He nodded. Tears were slipping from his eyes but he felt neither sorrow nor pain. "I just want to be alone for awhile." Jessie sniffled, and he realized she was crying. He kept his gaze on the closed blinds in the corner. "Please leave," he said.

He stared at the blinds until she gathered her things and slipped out the door.

"She's dead," he said aloud.

And now as he lay on the floor of the cabin, his shattered leg screaming in pain, he said it again. "She's dead." And she had been dead for over five years. And Harvey had been dead for two months. And Nicky. And Carly.

He rolled onto his stomach and pulled himself across the hardwood toward the dining room. He could barely see the patio doors in the darkness, and the drifts of snow piled against them. He inched closer, passing the dining table and his dead laptop, and the tile was cold against his belly and forearms.

With considerable effort, he managed to unlock the door and slide it back. Snow from the drift fell in upon him. He shook his head, knocking most of it off his hair and face, but burrowing it down beneath his shirt collar. He shivered violently as the cold wet trickled down his neck.

The snow was high, much higher than the dining room floor, and wriggling out onto the deck seemed impossible at first. The cold enveloped him like an icy cocoon as he pushed through the snow across the deck. He had no idea if he was going the right direction, or how far it was to the steps. All he knew was that he had to keep moving. Pushing. Plowing through the snow.

In mere seconds, his sweatshirt was soaked through, and his body was wracked with shivers. He pressed onward. Snow was in his eyes, his ears, his mouth. Cold and wet. It clumped in his hair and made its way down into his shirt, his jeans. Stuck to his sock-clad feet. And just when he thought he could go on no longer, he reached the edge.

The steps were a smooth incline down to the yard, with barely a ripple to show what lay beneath the snow.

Below, the hazy gray figures had gathered, watching him. Or as much as they could watch him without eyes. And that made him giggle like a madman.

A line from the Poe book sprang into his mind: *Yet, mad am I not – and very surely do I not dream.*

"I'm not mad!" he screamed at them. "I'm not mad!"

His hand pierced through the snow one last time, and too late he realized he'd gone out too far. He tumbled forward down the steps, wondering why the wooden slats were so hard when they were covered with such a deep cushion of snow.

A sound, halfway between a snap and a pop, reverberated through his neck and head, and the pain in his leg and hip ceased.

He came to rest at the bottom of the steps in a jumbled heap, facing upward toward the black sky. But it wasn't completely black. Dark gray clouds drifted across, and fine snowflakes hit his eyes, making him blink. He was covered in snow. He should be freezing, but he could feel nothing except a growing throb on the side of his face. He vaguely remembered knocking his head against the railing on the way down.

He lay looking at the sky, watching as the figures drew closer to him, as they surrounded him, as they gazed down at him with their sightless eyes.

And then they were upon him.

From the Springfield Clarion, *January 19:*

AUTHOR FOUND DEAD

A local author who once taught at Cedar Hill College and achieved fame with his Max Plexico children's book series was found dead at his family's summer home at Harper's Lake.

An autopsy showed Lee Houston, 39, died of carbon monoxide poisoning. Authorities said carbon monoxide was at lethal levels inside the home and was most likely caused by a faulty gas furnace.

Houston's wife, WSPR news anchor Jessica Houston, said her husband left Saturday to go to the family's cabin at Harper's Lake to work on a new project. After Tuesday's blizzard she became worried when she was unable to contact him and she reached out to the Lake County Sheriff's Office for help. Deputies entered the home Thursday morning and found Houston's body in an upstairs bedroom.

Deputy Chad Tribble, spokesman for the Sheriff's Department said Houston probably died some time Saturday night, just hours after entering the house.

"It's a heartbreaking situation," Tribble said, "but as good a time as any to remind folks to keep a working carbon monoxide detector in their home."

Houston shot to fame several years ago when his children's book series about an adventure-loving preteen, Max Plexico, hit the bestseller lists. Four of the books were turned into blockbuster films starring Justin Alexander.

Producer Marty Soebels, whose Dionysus Studios produced the Max Plexico films, said the loss of Lee Houston is a real tragedy. "He will be greatly missed," Soebels said in a press release. "His contribution to children's literature and entertainment was of a level only a few can ever hope to achieve. Our hearts and prayers go out to his family and friends."

Houston will be laid to rest tomorrow at Great Oaks Memorial Gardens in Springfield.

ACKNOWLEDGEMENTS

Thanks to my proofreaders/beta readers, Tracy Overby and Tony Furtado. Writing can be an isolating experience, so having people to bounce ideas off of and check over my work is a godsend. I'd also like to thank all the writers and instructors at the WMG Publishing Master Class in Lincoln City, Oregon, who welcomed me as one of their own and got me through my first West Coast workshop. It was great to be among "my people," and I hope to see you guys again!

W.D.O.
Owensboro, Kentucky
July 24, 2016

ABOUT THE AUTHOR

Will Overby has spent thirty years in the boardrooms and glass offices of retail banking. Between dodging mergers and drafting policies he publishes novels.

He lives along the Ohio River in western Kentucky where mysteries still abound and the tradition of storytelling is as strong as ever.

A graduate of Indiana University, Will is an avid Hoosiers football fan.